"Dance with me, Becka."

Her heart clattered against her rib cage. "Too risky."

"Okay, then. You asked for it." Giving a quick yank, he unbalanced her, plunging her into his lap. His arms went around her, he snuggled her against his chest and grinned down into her face. "Gotcha."

She struggled, but not nearly enough. While the sensible portion of her mind said get up and run, every other cell in her body refused to obey. Jett's cologne drifted up from his cotton T-shirt. His firm thighs pressed against her trapped fingertips, and she could scarcely keep from stroking them.

"When you turn me loose you're going to be very sorry," she said with more authority than she felt.

"Then I guess I might as well enjoy this while I can," he said as his blue eyes drifted over her face, coming to rest on her mouth.

"Don't even think about it, cowboy."

"Oh, I've been thinking about it a lot, and now I'm going to do something about it."

Dear Reader,

When you're stuffing the stockings this year remember that Silhouette Romance's December lineup is the perfect complement to candy canes and chocolate! Remind your loved ones—and yourself—of the power of love.

Open your heart to magic with the third installment of IN A FAIRY TALE WORLD…, the miniseries where matchmaking gets a little help from an enchanted princess. In *Her Frog Prince* (SR #1746) Shirley Jump provides a rollicking good read with the antics of two opposites who couldn't be more attracted!

Then meet a couple of heartbreaking cowboys from authors Linda Goodnight and Roxann Delaney. In *The Least Likely Groom* (SR #1747) Linda Goodnight brings us a risk-taking rodeo man who finds himself the recipient of lots of tender loving care—from one very special nurse! And Roxann Delaney pairs a beauty disguised as an ugly duckling with the man most likely to make her smolder, in *The Truth About Plain Jane* (SR #1748).

Last but not least, discover the explosive potential of close proximity as a big-city physician works side by side with a small-town beauty. Is it her wacky ideas that drive him crazy—or his sudden desire to make her his? Find out in *Love Chronicles* (SR #1749) by Lissa Manley.

Watch for more heartwarming titles in the coming year. You don't want to miss a single one!

Happy reading!

Mavis C. Allen
Associate Senior Editor

Please address questions and book requests to:
Silhouette Reader Service
U.S.: 3010 Walden Ave., P.O. Box 1325, Buffalo, NY 14269
Canadian: P.O. Box 609, Fort Erie, Ont. L2A 5X3

The Least Likely Groom

LINDA GOODNIGHT

SILHOUETTE *Romance*®

Published by Silhouette Books

America's Publisher of Contemporary Romance

For Celeste, Missy and Alison,
the best daughters-in-law on the planet.

And with special thanks to Super Bowl Champion
tight end Ernie Conwell for sharing his injury,
surgery and rehab information. Go Saints!

SILHOUETTE BOOKS

ISBN 0-373-19747-0

THE LEAST LIKELY GROOM

Copyright © 2004 by Linda Goodnight

Visit Silhouette Books at www.eHarlequin.com

Printed in U.S.A.

Books by Linda Goodnight

Silhouette Romance

LINDA GOODNIGHT

A romantic at heart, Linda Goodnight believes in the traditional values of family and home. Writing books enables her to share her certainty that, with faith and perseverance, love can last forever and happy endings really are possible.

A native of Oklahoma, Linda lives in the country with her husband, Gene, and Mugsy, an adorably obnoxious rat terrier. She and Gene have a blended family of six grown children. An elementary school teacher, she is also a licensed nurse. When time permits, Linda loves to read, watch football and rodeo, and indulge in chocolate. She also enjoys taking long, calorie-burning walks in the nearby woods. Readers can write to her at linda@lindagoodnight.com.

All underlined places are fictitious.

Chapter One

It had been a quiet summer Sunday in the small hospital of Rattlesnake, Texas…until a certain ornery cowboy appeared in the emergency room.

And now the misguided drunk-and-disorderly was singing at the top of his lungs.

From her spot at the nurses' desk, Rebecka Washburn placed a hand over the telephone receiver and frowned down the long, white-tiled corridor toward the holding area where he lay sprawled on a gurney. She glimpsed one dusty cowboy boot and a muscled, jean-covered leg before a nurse's assistant wheeled him into an exam room.

A tortured mangle of "He's Got the Whole World in His Hands" and a rodeo song about bulls and blood and dust and mud echoed through the corridor.

"Do what you have to, Sid," she said to the man on the other end of the line. "I'll rake up the money somewhere."

With a worried sigh she muttered her thanks to the town's only auto mechanic and replaced the receiver. Where was she going to get that kind of money?

The singing maniac ripped into a third, even heartier, chorus of the children's church song.

Determined to muzzle her unwanted serenader before he disrupted the other twenty patients on her wing, Becka pushed the nagging worry about her on-its-last-legs car into the background and padded on soft-soled shoes toward the E.R.

As charge nurse for the day shift, keeping everything running smoothly and under tight control was her responsibility. Control was what she did best. Every chart was neatly updated and in its proper slot, every medication carefully accounted for, and every patient given the best care a small-town hospital could manage. That included quieting down any and all drunks that passed through the doors.

"'He's got the little bitty babies in his hands,'" the man sang.

Irresponsible drunks. Didn't they understand, as she did, that even a few beers at the wrong time could be deadly? For the past three years she'd had to live with the horror of learning that the hard way, and every time a drunk showed up in her E.R., the memory returned in full force.

Face set in a stiff, professional mask, she pushed the pneumatic door open. A swoosh of cool, antiseptic air wafted out.

"Would you please stop that caterwauling before you send someone into cardiac arrest?"

A vaguely familiar cowboy was propped on the exam

table. His hat was askew. His black western shirt was filthy, and a wide abrasion marred his high, handsome cheekbone.

Becka clenched her teeth. So he was not only drunk and disorderly, he'd been fighting, too.

Hushed by her sharp command, the cowboy looking momentarily abashed. Then his glazed gaze roamed over her and a wicked little grin split his face.

"Well, lookie here, Jackson," he said to the tall, silent cowboy standing beside him. "It's the queen of the rodeo."

The man called Jackson removed his white Resistol and grinned, too. "I don't think so, Jett. Looks more like a little, mad redheaded nurse to me."

"A nurse? What's a nurse doing out here at the rodeo?" Mr. drunk-and-disorderly wobbled up from the gurney, his muscles rippling, his crystal-blue eyes showing alarm. The process knocked his black hat to the floor. "Did somebody get hurt?"

Becka captured his flailing arm and reseated him. Rock-hard muscle swelled beneath her fingers before the singing cowpoke collapsed wearily onto the pillow. With a moan he grabbed his head with both hands.

"I can't make my head be still," he mumbled.

"This is not a rodeo arena, cowboy, and it's no wonder your head is spinning. How much have you had to drink today?"

Both men turned curious faces toward her. Her patient looked more stupefied than curious.

"Have we been drinking, Jackson?" he asked, frowning.

"Nope."

"Didn't think so." His head wobbled crazily from side to side. "We haven't done that in a while, have we?"

"Nope."

"Then what's she so mad about?"

"I don't think she likes your singing."

"Oh, for goodness' sake." Becka huffed in exasperation. No doubt this wasn't his first visit to a hospital, and common sense said the E.R. was serious business. But when had any drunk shown common sense?

"If he hasn't been fighting, why is he here?"

"A bull didn't take too kindly to his showboating."

"A bull?" Becka came to full alert, her irritation washed away in a sea of guilty concern. "He's been in a rodeo accident?"

"Why else would we be in an emergency room on Sunday evening?"

"Good heavens."

Guilt sliced through her with the strength of a bone saw. She was a good nurse. A compassionate, go-the-extra-mile nurse, but this time she'd allowed painful personal memories to interfere with her job. Instead of recognizing an obvious concussion, she had jumped to the conclusion that he'd been drinking.

Would that awful day from her past ever stop haunting her?

Hustling to the blood-pressure monitor hanging on the wall, Becka pulled it down and wrapped the length of cloth around the man's well-developed biceps. Her patient had the typical body of a professional rider, athletic and strong enough to stay on a writhing bull, but not overly large. He had what she would term the perfect body—if she were interested in such things, that is.

"Tell me exactly what happened," she said to the tall cowboy called Jackson.

The injured man lay back, quiet for the moment, his eyes closed. A crooked little bump atop his nose suggested this wasn't his first rodeo injury, though his was still an incredibly attractive face, the kind of good-looking hunk of cowboy that had women lining up. She'd seen him somewhere before, she was certain. A woman didn't forget a face like that.

"He took a head butt from the back. Got his bell rung."

Becka filed that away. A two-thousand-pound bull could pack a real wallop. "And?"

The big guy shrugged. "And he toppled over like a hundred-pound feed sack."

Wincing at the unpleasant image, Becka pumped the sphygmomanometer bulb, listened for the familiar *thump-thump* while watching the needle dance rhythmically down to zero. His pressure was okay.

She reached for his pulse. Deeply ingrained calluses and the more recent red stripes of rope burn crossed the palm of his leatherlike hands.

She pursed her lips in disapproval. Like every rodeo cowboy she'd ever met he had no sense at all. Living on the edge, throwing caution to the wind, endangering himself and those around him.

"How long was he unconscious?"

"Unconscious? Me?" The cowboy on the table opened bleary eyes and struggled up on his elbows. "Never fainted in my—" He melted onto the pillow like hot wax.

The man called Jackson grimaced and shook his head. "Out like a light."

Someone pecked at the door. Then without waiting, an admissions clerk entered. She thrust some papers toward the tall cowboy hovering over the gurney. "Are you the patient's next of kin?"

"No ma'am. Jett is my traveling partner. We look after each other. But his brother lives around here if we need him."

"Becka," the woman asked. "Can he still sign the E.R. papers? Or do we need to wait on Mr. Garrett to wake up?"

"Garrett? Jett Garrett?" Memory flooding back, Becka turned toward the unconscious patient. "I remember him."

No wonder he'd looked familiar. He and her husband had played some rodeos together when she and Chris first started dating five years ago. Even Chris, as fearless as he was, marveled at Jett's reckless daredevil attitude.

"He's Colt Garrett's little brother. The wild and crazy one." The man was renowned for his careless, throw-caution-to-the-wind antics.

Jackson grinned. "One and the same. He and Colt own the Garrett Ranch outside of town. You know them?"

Reluctant to reveal just how she remembered Jett, Becka settled for the easy answer. "In a town of 6500 people, everyone knows everyone else, at least by name. Colt's wife, Kati, takes care of my son in her day care."

"'Do, Lord, oh, do, Lord…'" Jett's head wobbled back and forth on the pillow as he started singing in that deep baritone again. "'Where the buffalo roam and the bulls and blood and dust and mud…'"

His partner laughed out loud.

"You gotta admit, ma'am, he's pretty funny."

Becka suppressed a smile. "Does he always sing—and I use the word loosely—when he's injured?"

"Sings in his sleep, too. But never like this."

Becka ran experienced fingers through the dark wavy hair covering Jett's skull, searching for bumps or wounds. Finding none, she made the notation on the chart and reached for the telephone hanging on the wall next to the door. After a moment she hung up and turned toward the two men.

"Dr. Clayton will be here in a few minutes, but he said to go ahead and admit Jett for observation. Can't be too careful with a concussion—which he clearly has."

"Nope." Jett sat up as quickly as a jack-in-the-box, steadied himself with a hand on either side of the table, and shook his head. After two shakes his eyes crossed. "I appreciate the invite, but I can't stay."

Becka saw what he was about to do, but couldn't move fast enough to stop him from pushing off the table. He crumpled like a paper sack. The only thing that kept him from slamming onto the hard tile was the fast reflexes of his oversize friend.

"Whoa, there, partner." Jackson gripped his arms and hoisted up as Becka rushed to roll a wheelchair beneath him. "I think you better do what this little nurse tells you to."

Head lolling crazily, Jett gripped it with both hands and steadied the wobbling. "Nope, sorry, can't do it. I promised Melissa…"

For once in her career Becka was actually glad to see a patient pass out. Jett and his women were legend, and she really didn't care to hear about the latest flame.

While lifting his feet onto the wheelchair's foot support, she saw what she'd missed before.

"Good grief." Dropping to her knees beside the chair, she yanked a pair of bandage scissors from her uniform pocket.

"What?" Jackson squatted beside her.

"No wonder he passed out when his feet touched the floor."

Quickly cutting Jett's jean leg up the inner seam, she exposed the dark-muscled knee and thigh. The notion flickered through her head that he would be this rich tan color all over his body, a notion she squelched instantly. Jett needed her expertise, not her admiration, though heaven knew it was hard not to admire such an athletic, blatantly masculine body. Her husband's body had been like this, all hard-cut muscle without an ounce of fat.

But even Chris's perfect, athlete's physique hadn't been strong enough to stand up against the damage she'd unwittingly done it.

The familiar pain of guilt and loss twisted in her stomach. She glued her attention to Jett's injury. She could help Jett. She couldn't do a thing to help Chris. Not now. Not even then.

To her dismay, Jett's knee looked more like a softball than a body part. Gently running expert fingers over the hot, misshapen flesh, Becka chastised herself for missing so obvious an injury. She hadn't handled anything right today. Between the worry over her car, the nagging fear for her son's safety, and these unwanted reminders of her dead husband, she wasn't thinking straight at all.

"Oh, man," Jackson murmured. "The bull must have stepped on him."

"This had to hurt. Didn't he complain?"

Jackson shrugged. "Cowboys believe if you're still breathin' you ain't hurt."

"Then why'd you bring him to the E.R.?"

A grin split the big man's face. "I didn't want him to quit breathin'."

Becka shot him an exasperated look.

"The doctor will have to X-ray him and probably do a scan to say for certain, but I've seen this kind of injury before. He won't ride on this knee for a while."

"Jett won't like that. He's only a few rodeos away from the big show."

"Excuse me?"

"Vegas. Jett's never made it to the National Finals, but he has a shot this year. A few more rodeos, a few more points, and he's eligible."

Becka gave him a doubtful twitch of one eyebrow. "I don't like to rain on anyone's parade…."

"That bad, huh?"

"I'm afraid it could be."

They both stared at the unconscious patient. One with sympathetic eyes. The other with thoughts that the idiot would be better off in traction than to risk his life on the back of a Brahma bull.

Jett awakened that evening with the mother of all headaches. Turning only his eyes because his brain undulated like the curves of a belly dancer, he spotted an overhead television, a bedside table and a wheelchair. He eased his eyelids down again, waited two beats and tried again. He could not be where he thought he was.

"A hospital?" He ran a thick tongue over dry lips. His mouth tasted like the floor of a rodeo arena.

From the corner Jackson unwound his big body from a miserable-looking plastic chair. "You awake?"

"Must be talking in my sleep. I can't be in a hospital."

"Rattlesnake Municipal. At least for tonight."

A little quiver of relief shuddered through him. He was only here for the night. He must not be hurt too badly. Tomorrow he and Jacks would be back on the road. With a win in Odessa tomorrow night, he'd be one rodeo closer to the NFR.

"Did you bring me in here?"

"Yep. But Colt will be back in the morning to take you to Amarillo."

"Colt?" Jett frowned. What did his brother have to do with anything? "Amarillo?" Jackson was talking in riddles. Maybe he'd been the one to get his head dinged. "We're riding in Odessa tomorrow night, not Amarillo."

The brown door swished open and the tiniest redheaded nurse Jett could imagine whipped into the room. If she hadn't been wearing pink scrubs and a name badge that said, B. Washburn, RN, Jett would have sworn she was a little kid.

She bent over his knee, turning her backside in his direction.

Nope, he thought with an appreciative grin. This one's definitely not a kid. He was in the midst of a rather nice perusal of her other petite but womanly assets when she laid an ice pack against his leg.

Pain, violent enough to be rated F5 in the tornado world, shot from his kneecap to his head and rattled around inside his brain long enough to make him forget his name.

He clamped down hard on the inside of his cheek to keep his big mouth from squealing like a stuck hog. He'd had pain before, didn't really even mind pain that much since it was an expected part of his job, but this wasn't regular pain. This was hot-metal-in-the-eye pain. Steel-toed-boot-in-the-groin pain. Hold-me-down-and-stomp-my-nose pain.

The little nurse looked up with sympathetic eyes. "Would you like me to ask Dr. Clayton if you can have something for the pain?"

"Pain?" he grunted, sucking in air through his teeth. "I don't need anything for pain. What I need is my pants."

She cast a sideways glance at Jackson who looked way too serious. And Jacks was not a serious kind of guy. All of a sudden, Jett had a real bad feeling.

"Did something terrible happen to my pants?"

Jackson laughed. "Yeah. She cut 'em off."

"She did?" The dynamite blast in his leg had subsided a little. He managed a lascivious grin in the nurse's direction. "And what did she do to me while I was helpless and naked?"

B. Washburn, RN, never even blushed. Guys must come on to someone as cute as she was all the time.

Was that what he was doing? Coming on to her?

Nah. He couldn't afford to let himself get distracted right now with the NFR within reach. But she *was* cute.

Maybe later.

"So how am I going to get out of here without any pants?"

A cute little dip formed between Nurse Washburn's eyes. "Don't you remember talking to Dr. Clayton?"

That bad feeling came back, stronger this time. He cast a glance toward Jackson, who once more wore a troubled expression.

"'Fraid not. What's up?"

"We're sending you to Amarillo tomorrow to an orthopedic surgeon."

"For a headache?" He refused to think about that teensy-weensy twinge in his knee.

"At the very least, you have a severed ACL that will require surgery."

"How bad?" He looked to his partner for reassurance, but Jackson got that hang-dog look again.

Ignoring the incessant school of sharks ripping through his kneecap, he thought he'd better listen to Miss B. Washburn, RN, considering how he didn't recall ever meeting Dr. Clayton. Or having an MRI for that matter.

What she had to say really put a kink in his good mood. He knew all about tears of the anterior cruciate ligament. Every athlete hated them because they sidelined a guy too long. But from the way B. Washburn, RN, told it, a regular ACL tear didn't sound so bad. His, on the other hand, was way beyond torn. His knee was, as she so blatantly phrased it, "demolished."

"So, when can I ride again?" He asked when she finished telling him that not only was his dream in jeopardy, but his career, as well.

"That will be for the orthopod to say after he's done a scope."

Orthopod? Was that a doctor from outer space?

He thought better of asking. And to tell the truth, if someone didn't get the sharks off his leg, he was going to lose his sense of humor.

"But you'll be off the circuit for at least a couple of months, maybe longer."

"No way." He struggled up to his elbows. "Get me some pants, Jacks. I can ride."

To prove his point, he swung his right leg over the side of the bed, but the left one refused to follow.

B. Washburn, RN, caught him by the calf and pushed him gently, but efficiently back onto the bed. The eyes he'd thought of as honey-colored, now looked muddy with anger.

"Don't be foolish, Mr. Garrett. It's bad enough to put yourself in harm's way by riding bulls, but refusing treatment for severe injury is totally irresponsible. It won't heal and you won't ride, maybe ever again if you make it any worse."

He gazed down in amazement at her slender arms. "Hey, you're pretty strong for a girl."

She'd tossed him back onto the bed as easily as Sinsation had tossed him on his head. Dadgum ornery bull. "You must know judo or something."

"Or something." She favored him with a cheeky grin that sent a little spiral of interest curling through his belly. Darn if she wasn't making him think of taking a couple days off to hang around Rattlesnake and find out just what that something was—among other things.

"Man, what's the world coming to? I get stomped by a bull and body-slammed by a girl all in one day." Moving had stirred the knee-eating sharks, and he was starting to feel grouchy again. "Are you gonna get my pants or do I have to call 911 and report a theft, as well as a kidnapping?"

B. Washburn, RN, pushed the phone toward him. He

scowled at her. She stared back with those honey-colored eyes, as solemn and sympathetic as an undertaker. The real bad feeling settled in to stay. He got the unmistakable impression that he was about to take an unplanned vacation to Amarillo.

Chapter Two

Near the end of her shift Becka slid into a chair at the nurses' desk to make final notations on the patients' charts. As she leafed through Jett Garrett's, she frowned.

Rolling her chair away from the desk, she called to the nurse standing inside the medication room directly behind her. "Mindy."

"Yeah?" A bubbly blond head peeked around the door.

"Has Mr. Garrett in 14B had anything at all for pain since admission?"

"I haven't given him anything. Did you give him something in the E.R.?"

Becka worried her bottom lip and looked through the chart once more. "No."

"Those rodeo cowboys are so tough."

Becka rolled her eyes. Tough or not, the man had to hurt, and there was no way he could sleep with a roaring headache and a throbbing knee. As uncomfortable as she was around a man as reckless as Jett, tonight he was her responsibility and, bull rider or not, she would never shirk her duty. Neatly replacing the chart, she stashed the ink pen in the pocket of her scrubs and headed for room 14B. On the way she made up a new ice pack for his knee.

As she approached the room she heard the sounds of "Itsy Bitsy Spider" and didn't even try to stop the grin that formed on her lips. Her son, Dylan, loved that song and she'd tickled her fingers up his four-year-old arm a thousand times or more. Besides, Jett's inappropriate singing amused her.

Upon entering the room, Becka noticed at once that the cowboy was in a world of hurt: eyes squeezed a little too tight for sleep; lines of stress creasing his richly tanned forehead and bracketing the handsome mouth. The singing, no doubt, was to take his mind off the pain.

"'Down came the rain,'" he sang through gritted teeth.

"Mr. Garrett," she said softly.

The singing stopped. His eyelids sprang open. "Jett."

"All right, Jett. I have a new ice pack for your knee."

"Bring it on. The old one's lost its zip." He started up on one elbow, the sheet sliding down to reveal a sprinkle of black hairs on a brown, well-honed chest. Halfway up he grimaced and slid back onto the pillow.

"Would you like something for pain? Dr. Clayton left orders for an injection if you need it."

"A shot?" The apprehensive way he asked nearly had her laughing.

"It will ease the pain. I promise."

"I'm all right."

"You'll be better if you don't play macho man. The physiology of the human body is such that healing takes place much quicker if the muscles are relaxed. Yours are as a tight as the lid on a pickle jar."

He perked up. Cocking an eyebrow, he smoothed one hand over his six-pack belly. "Been looking at my muscles, huh?"

Becka ignored the little zip of interest. "They're stellar, I'm sure. Now why don't you let me get that injection for you so you can rest better?"

"On one condition."

She eyed him warily. With a wild man like Jett, a woman never knew what "condition" he might think of. "What's that?"

He indicated the green vinyl chair next to the bed. "You sit here by me afterward and talk to me until the medicine takes effect."

Surprised, Becka studied a pair of eyes so blue the sky dimmed in comparison. Was this a come-on from a guy accustomed to having his way with any and all women? Or was Jett Garrett, daredevil deluxe, afraid?

The question intrigued her. A glance at her watch revealed her shift would be over in fifteen minutes. She had to go by Sid's Repair Shop and check on her car before picking up Dylan at day care, so she couldn't stay later than that. One of the other nurses had offered her a ride— an offer she couldn't refuse under the circumstances.

However, except for Jett's, all the patient charts were signed out, and everything was in order and ready for the next shift to take over.

"I only have about fifteen minutes," she said. "But I'll stay that long."

"Deal." He closed his eyes again and lay back.

She stood there a moment, staring down at a too-handsome man with all the qualities that scared her to death. Restless and unpredictable, Jett lived his life on the edge, ever searching for the next thrill, never staying in one place or with one woman because something else always caught his quicksilver interest. Beyond fearless, wildly exciting, and every inch a man, Jett Garrett exuded an energy, a life force so powerful that he was in danger of burning himself out like a shooting star. And the fool didn't even know it.

But she knew. Oh, yes, Becka knew, for she had been a willing participant while another man's flame was extinguished by his own lust for life.

Other than the compassion that made her an excellent nurse, she had no explanation for why she'd agreed to spend an extra fifteen minutes just sitting beside the disturbing cowboy. Sure, she'd done it a hundred times for other patients, but this one was dangerous. Everything about him brought back painful memories that were always just below the surface struggling to rise up and choke her.

Her son's small, impish face flashed in her head. Dylan. Her heart squeezed painfully. What if she wasn't cautious enough and the careless genes that were as much a part of her makeup as they were Chris's resurfaced in him? What if something happened to him, too?

Jett's lips moved. "You gonna get that shot or kiss me?" He opened lazy eyes and grinned. "Either one is okay with me."

Disturbed at her troubled thoughts Becka yanked in a startled gasp and swept out of the room, cheeks hot.

Jett Garrett was the kind of man she avoided at all costs. He was dangerous. She knew his kind. Had suffered the consequences of being too enamored with the aura of excitement such men wore like others wore aftershave. Jett Garrett terrified her.

Then why had she experienced this funny little inner twinge when he'd mentioned kissing him? And why was her pulse suddenly racing along like freeway traffic?

Sliding moist palms down the sides of her scrubs, Becka pulled herself under tight control. Certainly, a man like Jett Garrett disturbed her; he was a reminder of things better left alone. But she was a professional. For Dylan's sake she had learned to handle anything.

She would go right back down to that room and give him the pain injection. She would sit down and talk to him. And she would not notice his perfect body or his handsome face or be affected by his sexy little quips. She would ignore the zip of excitement that threatened to undermine her safety. And by the time she returned tomorrow, Jett would be off to Amarillo and she'd never have to deal with him again.

An hour later when Becka pulled into the sunlit parking lot outside the day care center, she'd managed to push Jett Garrett out of her mind. Or rather Sid, the mechanic, had done the deed for her.

Shutting off the car key, Becka listened with a worried frown to a series of mysterious chugs before the engine wheezed into silence. Sid's words still rang in her ears.

"I'm not even sure I can get parts for this kind of car anymore. Give it up, Becka, before you get stranded again, or worse, have an accident."

And on those words she'd driven away, the old Fairlane patched together once more by the expertise of a kind mechanic, knowing full well she had to find a way to buy another vehicle—soon.

Getting out of the car, she opened the gate to the fenced facility and started up the sidewalk toward Kati's Angels Day Care. The name always made her smile because Kati Garrett, the owner and proprietress, did indeed treat each of her charges like gifts from Heaven. A very protective mother, Becka was thankful to have the serene and loving Kati caring for Dylan.

Inside the long open room, she spotted her son immediately. In the company of three other preschoolers, he ran in frenzied circles around a stack of wooden blocks and toy trucks, making car noises and issuing pretend honks.

Becka stared in disbelief. He shouldn't be running. He could fall. Hit his head. Be killed.

"Dylan!" she called sharply and started toward him. Anxiety gripped her.

Kati Garrett, having a pretend tea party at a low table with four little girls, rose at the sound of Becka's voice. Seven months' pregnant, she moved slowly, but her face was filled with concern.

Dylan, too, heard the fear in his mother's voice. He stopped dead still only to be pummeled from behind by an overzealous playmate and knocked to the floor. The action sent Becka into a lope. Heart beating crazily, she rushed to her fallen child and yanked him into her arms.

"Are you all right?" She heard the panic in her voice and knew it was entirely out of proportion to the incident, but she couldn't help herself. If anything happened to Dylan, she could not go on living. Not this time.

Dylan's lips quivered. Tears rimmed his wide, hazel eyes. "I sorry, Mommy. I sorry."

"Is he hurt?" Kati, now beside them, asked.

Becka did a quick once over, checking the child for injuries. "No. But he could have been. Why on earth was he allowed to run wild like that?"

"Becka, little boys are naturally rambunctious. It's a part of their physical makeup. Running is healthy. I can't make him sit in a chair all day."

Becka inhaled deeply then blew out a calming breath. "I know." She shook her head, embarrassed now that she knew her son was all right. "But it's dangerous for him to be so unruly."

Kati touched her arm and said quietly, "I was actually pleased to see him playing with such zest. Of all the little boys, Dylan is the most timid."

Kati's son, four-year-old Evan, dark eyes echoing his mother's concern, hurried over to them. "Is Dylan hurt, Mommy? I bumped him down."

Kati laid a hand on her son's smooth, brown hair. "He's fine, baby."

"I not a baby." He patted her bulging tummy with a chubby hand. "Baby is here."

Both women smiled indulgently. Becka hoisted Dylan higher on her hip. "Do you allow Evan to run and roughhouse that way?"

"Oh my, yes. At home he and his daddy wrestle and romp like two puppies. Colt had him on a horse by himself on his second birthday."

Becka shuddered at the thought. "How can you stand it? Aren't you afraid something will happen to him?"

Kati laughed and swooped Evan into her arms. "His

daddy loves him. Colt would never do anything to cause Evan harm."

When Kati spoke her husband's name, her eyes lit up. Becka envied the couple, though she was as amazed as everyone else in Rattlesnake when Colt, the confirmed bachelor with a reputation almost as bad as that of his brother, had married his quiet nanny and adopted the infant Evan. But anyone who'd seen the family together knew they had something special.

"How was Jett doing when you left the hospital?" Kati asked.

At Becka's look of surprise, she went on. "Colt came by earlier and told me. Is the knee as bad as he says?"

"Probably worse," Becka answered, remembering the way Jett had tried to downplay his injury.

"Probably. These cowboys, especially the Garrett men, think they are invincible." Kati smiled softly and shook her head, a dark, waist-length braid swaying. "Sometimes I think Colt actually is."

Becka wondered what it would be like to love a man the way Kati loved her husband. So confident. So secure. Yes, she'd loved Chris but not like this. Theirs had been a frenetic life, always on the edge, never safe and secure. She'd learned a valuable lesson from that short, manic episode of her life. Now, safety and security were the only things she wanted. That and a new car.

She sighed, weary with the constant worry over finances, and redirected her thoughts. "Your brother-in-law will get great care in Amarillo. If anyone can repair the damage to his knee, the orthopedic team there can."

"Colt said he had a concussion, too. Something about him singing his fool head off."

Becka laughed. "I've never seen anyone react to a head injury in such an entertaining way."

"That's Jett for you. Always doing the unexpected."

"Unexpected" Becka could do without. She didn't like surprises. She liked safe, routine, predictable. Come to think of it she hadn't seen Sherman Benchley, her occasional date, in a while. Maybe she'd give him a call and invite him over for a movie and popcorn tonight. With Sherman she always got exactly what she expected.

The unexpected occurred a week later. Called into the hospital's administrative office, Becka sat across the desk from the director of nurses, Marsha Simek. The two had worked together since Becka's graduate days shortly before Chris's death and shared a friendly, comfortable relationship.

"I received an interesting call today," Marsha said, fixing Becka with a curious blue gaze.

"Concerning me?"

"It seems you made quite an impression on one of our patients recently, and now he's interested in hiring you to do home health care visits."

Becka leaned forward, immediately interested. She'd done some home health care on the side to bolster her ever-low bank account, and right now she could certainly use some extra cash.

"Who was it? The man who had the foot amputation? Mr. Novotny?"

"No." Marsha shuffled some papers, came up with a yellow sticky note, and handed it to Becka. "Jett Garrett. Do you remember him?"

"Jett—" The words stuck in Becka's throat. Anyone

but the singing cowboy with enough masculine chemistry to melt paint. "Why would he need a home health nurse?"

"Seems he's staying out at that ranch he and his brother own while he recoups from knee surgery." Marsha crossed her arms on the desk. "The orthopedic docs in Amarillo sent him home with a PT machine and he's having fits trying to run it."

"I'm not a physical therapist."

"No, but you know enough about it to do the visits, help him with the machine, and see that he follows doctor's orders. The PT department could give you a quick in-service if you're not familiar with that particular piece of equipment."

"Why me? Why not send PT out?"

"They're too shorthanded. Besides, Mr. Garrett insisted on hiring you. And with your fitness training, coupled with nursing expertise, you're the obvious choice."

"Well, call him back and tell him I'm not interested."

Marsha looked surprised. "Not interested? Becka, the pay is excellent."

She didn't even want to know.

Marsha told her, anyway, naming a sum considerably more than her usual fee. She needed that money, needed it badly. But Jett Garrett? No way. She shivered with a sense of unease and a flutter of unwanted interest at the idea of spending time in his troubling presence.

"I can't, Marsha. Sorry." She stood to leave, anxious to get back to her station. The physicians should be making rounds anytime now and they'd be looking for her.

"How's your dad doing?"

She stuck a fist on one hip. "Dad's okay, but that was a dirty trick."

Marsha knew about Becka's money woes. About the ailing father whose social security check didn't cover his medications each month and about the hospital and funeral bills Becka was still paying off.

"Now Becka, what would it hurt to work for this guy for a few weeks? Make the money, make the hospital look good, help a patient. Everybody wins."

Everybody but Becka. Hand on the door she blew out a long, exasperated breath. "I'll think about it."

She thought about it all day long, pulling the yellow sticky note out of her pocket a dozen times to stare at the name and phone number. By shift's end, she'd reaffirmed her decision. She couldn't take the chance. No matter that the money would go a long way toward a down payment on another car she absolutely, positively would not work for Jett Garrett.

Collecting her purse from the employee lounge, she soft-soled down the anesthetic-scented corridors and out to the parking lot. Her neck and shoulder muscles ached and the beginnings of a headache tapped at the base of her skull. Tension. Pure and simple.

Last night Dylan had somehow managed to open the front door by himself and had gone out into the yard without her knowledge. Finding her son gone when she got out of the bathtub had shaken her to the core. She'd found him playing not ten feet from the busy residential street. Her yard needed a fence, but fences cost money. She'd simply have to be more careful. Maybe a lock higher up on the door would do the trick.

Her baby boy was getting more adventurous by the

day and the idea unnerved her. She'd tried her best to squelch this side of him, warning him of impending disaster but he hadn't slowed down one bit. Her father warned that she'd make him a sissy, but Dad didn't understand. He'd been a dirt track racer in his younger days before the diabetes damaged his vision, and he thought a man wasn't a man unless he took chances. Just because a child still sucked his thumb and sometimes wet the bed didn't make him a sissy. And even if it did, he would be alive.

Still, last night's episode coupled with today's tempting but impossible job offer from Jett Garrett had made this a stressful day.

Climbing into the old white Fairlane, Becka cranked the engine. The starter ground predictably, then a series of *pop, pop, pops* issued from the tailpipe. Acrid-smelling black smoke swirled in through the open window. All perfectly normal for her dying vehicle except for one thing: this time the engine didn't start. She tried again, went through another series of smoky backfires and then—nothing. After several more attempts, she—and the car's battery—gave up.

The tapping in the back of her head turned to hammering. Grabbing her purse, she shoved her shoulder against the sticking door, stepped out onto the warm pavement and headed back inside the hospital to call Sid. Maybe the part required to fix the car had miraculously arrived today, though she had no idea how to pay for it.

No. That wasn't true. She knew how to pay for it. She was just too scared. As she trudged up the sidewalk, the yellow sticky note felt like a brick in her uniform pocket.

She was scared of Jett Garrett. Scared of the energy in him, of the things he made her remember, and most of all, scared of the way her made her feel.

But fear or not, she had no choice. She had to take that job.

Chapter Three

Fresh from a one-legged shower, Jett slipped on a pair of boxers and a T-shirt and eased down onto the side of the bed. He was out of breath from the effort, a fact that ticked him off no end. Since when did a little bitty knee injury turn a man into a wuss? Sure, he had a bolt poking out each side of his leg with a cagelike stabilizer bar attached, but that shouldn't make him so weak and winded. Nobody had warned him he'd come home with enough hardware attached to his leg to build a bucking chute.

He had to get over this thing. And soon. Time was passing. Rodeos were happening without him. The dream was fading like a new pair of Wranglers in hot water.

With more effort than he wanted to admit, he hoisted up and hobbled to the calendar on the wall. The National Finals were in December. This was mid-August. He flipped the pages, counting the weeks. He needed more wins, more rodeos to have enough qualifying points.

At the knock on the door behind him, he called, "Come on in."

Must be Cookie, the ranch's chief cook and bottle washer, though the old sailor seldom knocked. He barged in, blasting like a foghorn, usually grousing because Jett had left something in a mess. Jett screwed up his forehead, thinking. Probably the bathroom this time.

"I'll take care of it later," he offered.

"Should you be up on that leg?" a soft, feminine voice, nothing at all like Cookie's foghorn, asked. He felt an undeniable lift in his spirits. Nothing like a little tête-à-tête with the opposite sex to cheer a fella up.

Putting all his weight on the good leg, Jett pivoted around and let his gaze slide slowly over the small, uniform-clad woman decorating the entrance to his bedroom. Sure enough, B. Washburn, RN, the cute redheaded nurse with the sassy attitude had arrived.

He flicked a glance toward the clock radio on the nightstand in appreciation of her punctuality. It was three forty-five and she didn't get off until three. That's what she'd told him when they'd talked on the phone the other night. He'd enjoyed that conversation. Had flirted with her shamelessly in an effort to elevate his own lousy mood. She'd flirted a little herself, though she kept wanting to talk about the job. Imagine. Talking work when you could play.

She came on into the room, pretending to pay no heed to his general state of undress, though Jett was certain he detected a flicker of interest, quickly shuttered. He kept in good shape, knew he looked good, and if the ladies appreciated his body, all the better for him. He certainly knew how to appreciate a woman.

His spirits lifted a little more. He was bored stiff, ready for some kind of stimulus to keep him breathing until he could get back on the road. Nothing like a female to provide that—temporarily, of course. If there was one thing Jett Garrett did not believe in, it was permanency. No permanent job. No permanent home. And most certainly, no permanent woman. He shuddered at the thought of being tied down in one spot with one woman too long. This few-week detour was already making him nuts.

"Did you have any trouble finding the place?"

"You gave excellent directions—for a man." Offering him a smile to soften the jab, she set a small tote bag on the blue armchair next to the door and started digging through it.

Jett enjoyed the view. Body bent, trim behind pointed toward him, she did interesting things to a pair of ordinary purple scrubs. He'd never really appreciated that color before, but he was beginning to see its virtues.

"Speaking of directions," she said, "I brought some simplified instructions for using this machine of yours. I should be able to train you in its use and on the rehab exercises in a matter of days."

Not if he had his way, she wouldn't. He could be dumb when he needed to be.

"What's the *B* stand for?"

Straightening, she gave him a quizzical smile. "Pardon?"

He pointed to her name badge. "B. Washburn, RN."

On the phone she'd referred to herself as "Nurse

Washburn from the hospital," saying the words in a prissified voice that announced her intentions of maintaining a professional distance. But that wasn't going to happen. Professional was fine. Distance? Uh-uh.

She touched the pin above her left breast. "Becka. Rebecka, actually, but I prefer Becka. Shorter and easier."

"Becka-Rebecka. Suits you." His memories of the overnight stay in Rattlesnake Municipal were a little fuzzy, but he remembered her. Under the uptight exterior there might be a tiger in the tank. Be interesting to find out.`

"Come on over and sit down." She motioned toward the recliner Colt and Cookie had dragged into his bedroom. "I'll examine your leg, take your vitals, then get the PT machine started."

Left leg straight out in front, he gingerly lowered his body into the chair and motioned toward the mechanical device standing nearby. "Looks like something out of a medieval torture chamber, doesn't it?"

Amusement flared in her. "You know medieval history?"

"What? You think I'm stupid because I'm a cowboy?"

Kneeling before him, she ran expert hands over his knee then checked the pulse in the back. Darn, but he liked those feathery-light hands touching his skin.

"I think you're stupid because you ride bulls and risk killing yourself for a living."

He looked down at the top of her head, bent as she seriously examined all the places where rods and wires poked through his hide. Her hair was parted in the middle, a little crookedly, and pulled into a smooth ponytail that hung to her shoulder blades. He wondered how it would look hanging loose around her delicate face, then smiled to himself. He'd find out. Women were an adventure and a heck of a lot of fun as long as they didn't go getting serious on you.

"I don't ride bulls for a living. I ride for fun."

She harrumphed. "That's even dumber."

"Hey, don't knock it till you've tried it." He slapped a hand against his thigh. "Now there's an idea. Wanna learn to ride bulls? I'll teach you."

"You won't be doing much of anything for the next eight weeks."

"Four weeks tops." He didn't tell the rest. That he really planned to make the Stampede over in Albuquerque during Labor Day weekend less than three weeks away. The bolts would be out by then, replaced by an air splint, and if he could walk he could ride. "I got rodeos to make."

She tilted her head and looked at him. She had the most appealing golden flecks in her pale brown eyes. "You have a knee to heal. I'm a good nurse, Jett, but I don't do miracles. According to Dr. Jameson you need at least eight weeks of rehab, six hours a day before you even think about riding again. Anything less and you may never ride another bull—or even a horse for that matter."

"Then let's get it on." He motioned toward the PT equip. "Bring on the torture chamber."

"Looks like one of those space satellites to me."

He cocked his head sideways and studied the device. "Hey, you're right. Think we could pick up satellite TV? The OLN channel carries rodeo."

"Let's point you toward the southern sky and give it a try."

They both laughed as Becka went to work, easing his leg into a weird-looking harness, Velcroing him in, explaining as she went. He mostly ignored her words and concentrated on her efficient movements and on the way she smelled—which was pretty darn sexy for a woman who'd already worked all day.

"Are you tired?" he asked.

She glanced sideways without answering, and he wondered why he'd asked such a dumb question. She made one last adjustment, and turned the On dial, setting the machine into a slow in-and-out rhythm.

Jett gripped the side of the chair. The sharks were back. "Turn the stereo on, will ya?" he grunted.

"If that's too painful, I can adjust it for less tension." She reached for the power switch.

"I never said it hurt." He was no baby.

"You sure?"

"No pain, no gain." He sucked in a roomful of air and tried to relax. "Just turn the radio on and dance with me."

She rose from her position beside the machine and stared at him as if he'd lost his reason. "Is the concussion still giving you problems?"

"Nah. I'm just in the mood to dance with a pretty girl. Come on. Humor me. I'm a poor wounded cowboy." Angling his head toward the source of agony, he waggled his eyebrows in invitation. "One of my legs is already dancing. Might as well find a way to enjoy it."

He held out his arms. She backed away, but he didn't miss the leap of excitement in her eyes before she shook her head, and the uptight, rigid demeanor returned.

"I really have to be going."

"Going? You can't leave." He would die of boredom sitting in this spot for six hours without anything but the television to distract him. "You're my nurse. I hired you. You gotta dance with me."

Summoning up his most persuasive smile—no small feat considering the sharks in his knee—he reached out and caught her hand.

"Really, Jett. This is a professional visit, not a social one."

A horrible thought crossed his mind. "You're not married, are you?"

She shook her head. "No."

"Okay, then. No reason on the planet why we can't dance."

"As I said, this is a professional visit."

"So? Dancing is therapy."

Her lips twitched, and she didn't remove her hand. He thought he might be making progress.

"Therapy? Now how do you figure that?"

Slapping his free hand against his chest, he pretended shock. "What? A fine nurse like you has never heard of recreational therapy?"

She made a snorting sound but he could see she wanted to laugh. He pressed the advantage. "I'm suffering terribly here, Nurse Becka-Rebecka. You can take my mind off the pain." That much was certainly true. "Drag that chair over here."

Though her expression was suspicious, she did as he asked.

"Now what, Mr. Idea Man?"

"Push in that Garth Brooks CD, then sit down and let's dance."

"Well..." Shaking her head, she turned on the stereo and sat down. "I suppose it's harmless."

Jett had never danced from a chair before but the idea intrigued him. He'd danced in bed, underwater, and on snow skis, so why not in a chair while sharks ripped his kneecap off?

Somehow he managed to maneuver his upper body sideways, and when Becka laughed, he purposely contorted his body a little more. He placed one of her hands on his shoulder and clasped the other one against his chest. The action unbalanced Becka and she pitched forward, landing with a surprised "ooph" against his upper body.

Man, she smelled good. Like clean sheets. And he did love the scent of a woman between clean sheets.

For a second Becka struggled to right herself, but he held on, swaying to the strains of the old Garth Brooks tune "The Dance."

In too awkward a position to do otherwise, Becka rested her head against his shoulder. But where he'd hoped for a quick melting, she held herself rigid and restrained.

"Loosen up, Becka-Rebecka," he whispered against her ear. "Muscles must be relaxed for healing to occur. Didn't you teach me that?"

She tilted her face up toward his. "I thought you had a concussion that night."

He grinned down at her and shrugged. She laughed, visibly relaxing as though by some inner command. Jett used the opportunity to snug her close. A dirty trick, he knew, but he was an invalid after all, in need of therapy.

He peeked over her shoulder. By now she was reclining on the arm of his chair and leaning into him. He could deal with that. Why hadn't he tried chair dancing before?

"A little practice and we could take this routine on the road." He gave a sudden tilt to the side as though to dip her. When he brought her upright, she held on, arched her body and tossed back her head. He followed her in a very distorted imitation of Fred and Ginger swinging from side to side, dipping up and back.

"I can see it now in neon lights. The newest fad. Chair dancing." Her face was slightly flushed and her amber eyes sparkled.

"Guaranteed to cure what ails you." He forgot all about his screaming knee. "Good for aches and pains, warts and athlete's foot. Order now and get a second chair free."

She picked up the spiel. "Send your check or money order for $19.95. Hurry, this offer ends soon."

The music ended, much to Jett's displeasure, and his dance partner pulled away, righting herself on the chair next to him. All the fun faded from her expression and she looked as though she regretted their few moments of silliness.

"Well." Averting her eyes, she straightened her uniform. "I really do have to leave now. My son is in day care and Kati closes at six."

"You have kids?"

Her faced softened. "Dylan. He's nearly four."

So she had a son but wasn't married. He'd like to hear that story, but figured now, when she was about to run, wasn't the best time to pry.

"Call Kati. She can bring him out here when she comes home and you can stay and entertain me a while longer."

"I can't ask Kati to do that."

"I can. Hand me the phone."

"No. I have to go." She gathered up her tote and started talking about the PT machine again, giving him some last-minute instructions, reminding him to ice pack the incision after therapy. She seemed intent on re-gaining her professional footing.

"Hey," he called when she opened the door and moved to leave.

She turned.

He gave her what he hoped was his sexiest grin. "Thanks for the dance."

She responded with a look he couldn't begin to in-terpret, then closed the door behind her.

Jett flopped back into the chair, disappointed, the in-cessant hum of the machine annoying him.

What was happening here? He hadn't asked the woman to marry him. Heaven forbid. He'd only wanted a little diversion until he could get the heck out of Dodge.

Since when had any female ever walked out on Jett Garrett?

Man. He must be losing it.

"Chair dancing!" Teeth gritted, Becka thumped her forehead against the steering wheel. During the time she'd been inside the Garrett Ranch, the Texas sun had filled her on-the-road-again car with enough hot air to launch a balloon festival, but it was those few minutes of up-close-and-personal with Jett Garrett that had her in a sweat.

Less than an hour in the magnetic cowboy's presence and she'd lost all sense of decorum, behaving in an uncharacteristically unprofessional manner. What had come over her?

But she knew. The carefully sublimated side of herself that she worked so hard to control had leaped to the fore at the first opportunity. In fact, her blood still hummed, and pleasure still tingled her nerve endings. Jett had tapped into the reckless nature she wanted so much to destroy.

She'd intended to stay longer, to see that Jett tolerated the PT machine well and to observe for swelling but as soon as the music ended, she'd realized what was happening and knew she had to escape. She couldn't do this again. She'd have to find an excuse not to come back here. Jett was too dangerous. She couldn't take a chance at letting her own rash nature resurface.

But how? What excuse could she use? And what would she do without the money this job would provide?

"Ma'am," a deep voice said right next to her ear. Stewing over the concern, Becka hadn't heard the approaching footsteps.

She nearly jumped out of her skin. Raising her head from the steering wheel, she saw Jett's brother, Colt, peering in through her window.

"You all right?"

Quickly she rolled down the window, nodding. "Yes, of course." Like an idiot she was roasting alive in her own car, too caught up in her emotional response to Jett to even realize how hot she was.

Thinking fast, she said, "I was about to check the water in my radiator before I leave. Sometimes my car overheats."

She pulled on the door handle, waited for Colt to step back and then exited the car.

"I keep a five-gallon container of water in the back just in case."

Colt raised an eyebrow but didn't comment on that. "I'll check it for you."

Becka watched the tall cowboy pop the hood on her car and go through the motions of examining the water content. He was definitely Jett's brother, with his dark good looks, but where Jett was flip and carefree, Colt was more serious, having little to say.

While Becka stood by in the Texas heat, Colt added water to the radiator, replaced the cap, then slammed the hood.

Wiping his hands down the sides of his jeans, he turned to where she leaned against the battered fender of her ancient car. "My brother giving you any problem?"

Becka tried not to blush, but the heat rose in her face anyway. "No. Not at all."

"I want Jett to have the best care, whatever it costs." Colt studied her. "If he needs you here longer, I'd like you to stay. I'll pay extra if necessary."

Becka stiffened. Was he questioning her ability to do a professional job? A twinge of guilt shifted over her. Hadn't she just questioned that very thing? From the inappropriate way she'd reacted to Jett Garrett, she couldn't trust herself. Why should anyone else trust her? But she couldn't admit that to Colt.

"You can rest assured that I will give your brother the best of care, but I have to get back into town before six to pick up my son."

Colt stepped around her to replace the water container in her back seat. "Doesn't Kati keep your little boy?"

"Yes. And she's wonderful with him."

That made him smile. "Yeah. Kati's something."

Those few words coupled with the twinkle in his eye told her that the tough cowboy wasn't so tough when it came to his wife.

"Even a dedicated woman such as Kati likes to close up shop and come home at the end of a long day." Becka wrenched open the car door and slid inside, ready to leave. "It would be unfair of me to ask her to keep Dylan any longer."

"You can bring him out here with you if you'd like. Then you won't need to hurry off."

Becka's pulse set up another drum beat. Great. Just what she didn't need. An excuse to stay longer in the presence of Jett Garrett when she was already searching for a way out of the entire commitment.

"Actually, it's such a long way out here, I was thinking this may not work out for me."

"You tell Jett that?"

"Not yet."

"Don't." He leaned down into the window. "My brother has his heart set on making the NFR this year. I think he's crazy, but if he wants it, I want him to have it. He's getting on in years for a bull rider."

"Getting on in years?" she asked incredulously. There was nothing old about the hot hunk with the dark, muscled thighs and rippling belly whose crooked grin could incite naughty thoughts in an angel.

Colt shrugged. "Thirty-one isn't young in bull riding. This may be his last shot."

"I hope he makes it, then," she said lamely, really thinking Jett needed to be institutionalized for even considering riding another bull after what the last one had done to him.

"Yeah. Well, he's lazy sometimes. He'll need a nurse who can push him, make him stay off that knee, do the exercises, that sort of thing. I'd pay extra for that kind of care."

"The pay is sufficient already." Not that she couldn't use more, but fair was fair.

"But I want to ensure the kind of care that will keep you here as long as he needs you. Bring your son, stay as long as it takes to harass my brother back to good health, and find a nice bonus in each paycheck." He named a healthy sum that almost caused Becka to swoon. With that amount she could put a large down payment on a car.

Colt saw her hesitation. "How about it, then? We got a deal?" Eyebrows raised in question, he stuck out a leathery hand.

A shiver of foreboding crawled over Becka's flesh like a spider in the darkness. Even though the warning bells in her head clanged louder than a five-alarm fire, Becka was trapped. She was desperate for a new car.

Somehow, some way she had to spend every evening in Jett Garrett's sexy, masculine presence without losing control again.

Sealing her fate, Becka reluctantly joined her hand to Colt's.

She could do this. She could.

But she had no idea how.

Chapter Four

"Here she comes. Little thing, ain't she?"

Jett paused in his dart throw to look at Cookie, who'd come to his bedroom bearing pink lemonade and blueberry muffins. The old Navy man, tattoos covering his tree-trunk arms, stood at the window looking out at the driveway.

"Who?" Jett asked, though he knew very well who Cookie meant. About three-thirty every afternoon the tingle of awareness started down in his gut and didn't let up until Becka was long gone and he was exhausted from an overdose of exercise and agony.

Cookie laughed, an air horn blast that raised the hairs on Jett's arms. "You ain't fooling me, Jett Garrett. You've been as alert as Kati's cat for the last ten minutes waiting on that nurse to arrive."

"She's my ticket back to the circuit."

"Uh-huh. Whatever you say. Just don't be playing fast and foolish with her. She don't seem the type."

"Tell me about it." He was absolutely frustrated by Becka-Rebecka's lack of cooperation. Here he was, bored to the point of watching Oprah, dying of a knee injury, and she refused to entertain him even a little bit. He was going to change that tonight or fire her. Maybe.

For a week now, Becka-Rebecka had arrived on time, harassed him for several hours, tortured his knee, and looked as hot as the face of the sun. But every time he managed to break through her icy control, she pulled back and made some excuse to leave. That annoyed him. He knew she wanted to cut loose and have fun— suppressed passion screamed to escape—but for some weird reason she wouldn't let go.

She had a cute little boy, too, but she kept him as tied up in knots as she was. Nagging him to sit still and watch TV when he wanted to play outside with Evan or roam the house like a normal kid. Kati and Colt didn't mind, so why should Becka?

Cookie greeted B. Washburn, RN, as she came in, then scuttled out of the room with the promise of more muffins anytime she wanted them. Jett pretended to ignore her, but every cell in his body knew she had arrived. Man, he was in need of female company in the worst way.

Humming a few bars of "Old McDonald," he took aim at the dartboard and, at the refrain of ee-ii-ee-ii-oh, he let fly, hitting a bull's eye.

He clapped his hands. "Let's see you beat that one, Becka-Rebecka."

She set her bag on the chair. "You think I can't?"

He held a dart toward her. "You don't have a prayer."

A leap of interest lit her golden eyes, but instead of taking the proffered dart and rising to the challenge as she clearly wanted to do, she pulled out a blood pressure cuff. "We have work to do."

She wrapped the cuff around his arm and stuck the stethoscope in her ears.

Reaching up, he pulled one earpiece away and taunted, "Women are lousy at sports, anyway."

With hardly a twitch of an eyelash, she replaced the earpiece, pumped the machine, took the reading, and put the equipment in her bag. Disappointment crept over Jett. Dang it. Wasn't there any way to penetrate that calm of hers?

Maybe he *would* have to fire her.

Nah, the chances of getting Nurse Ratched or some ugly old bag were too high. At least Becka-Rebecka looked good. Smelled great, too—like sugar cookies. And since that first night, when he'd held her close and danced that absurd chair dance, he hadn't been able to stop thinking about her taut little body against his.

He reached for another dart, only to have it yanked from his fingers.

"Wait a minute there, cowboy," she said with a quirk of her lips. "My turn."

While he stared in pleased surprise, she took aim and drove the dart straight into the bull's-eye.

He dipped his chin in appreciation. "I'm impressed. Bet you can't do it again."

"Tell you what. Let's get this PT under way and I'll show you what a measly *female* can do."

Somehow with his taunt about females and sports, he'd struck a nerve with Becka.

Sweet. Very sweet. Anything to break her out of control mode.

Though he tempted her with another invitation to chair dance, she shook her head, but a tiny smile lifted her mouth. She had enjoyed that night whether she wanted to admit it or not.

"No dancing. Just darts."

"If you lose will you dance with me?" He really wanted to feel her in his arms again. A man got lonely watching reruns of the *Beverly Hillbillies*. Elly May could only do so much for a guy.

"I won't lose."

"But what if you do? What do I get?"

"What do I get if I win?"

Ah, now they were negotiating. Things were definitely looking up.

"What do you want?" Wagging his eyebrows, he stroked the front of his T-shirt. "Besides me, of course."

With a tilt of her head, she gave him a look that would have insulted a lesser man. "You lose, you do fifty extra leg presses."

"No way." In addition to the PT machine, she'd started him on a regimen of exercises that bordered on the sadistic.

She gave a shrug that said she didn't care whether they played darts or not, then poked a thermometer in his mouth.

"Okay," he said when she removed the thermometer. "Twenty-five."

Her lips curved into a victory smile, and Jett knew she'd outwitted him. "Deal."

While she attached him to the piece of equipment he

affectionately termed the shark machine, he sang a few bars of "Home, Home on the Range" to keep from behaving like a total wuss.

"The inventor of that machine got his ideas from the Spanish Inquisition," he grunted.

Becka frowned, watched him for a minute before making an adjustment. "Better?"

"Yeah." Slowly his knee began to acclimate to the agony. "Now hand me those darts."

She did. "I see Cookie left refreshments again."

"I think he has a crush on you."

"A girl could do worse."

"Cookie's twice your age." He threw a dart so hard it bounced off the board and clattered into the stereo cabinet.

"One down. Two to go." She retrieved the misguided missile. "I didn't say he was my type, but he is a nice man."

"Oh. Yeah. Cookie's the best." Lamenting the wasted dart, he threw two bull's-eyes in a row then slid a sideways glance in her direction. "What *is* your type?"

She left his side long enough to pluck the darts from the wall board. "Somebody safe and predictable."

"Boring." Though he cringed at the thought, he was relieved, too. Becka would never be interested long-term in a restless wanderer like him. Short-term, though, was right up his alley. "You gonna throw those darts or declare a forfeit?"

"You wish," she said, then nailed all three darts into the bull's-eye.

He enjoyed the way she concentrated, the way her tiny pink tongue poked out the corner of her sexy, kissable mouth when she focused, and the flex of the cutest biceps muscle he'd ever seen.

"Pretty nice bicep for a girl."

"Are you ignoring the fact that a girl has now beaten you at darts?"

"Nope. Just admiring your muscle. Can I feel?"

Following a funny look that asked what he wanted to feel, she flexed her arm. An amazing muscle popped up.

"You must work out. Or does throwing patients around in bed do that for you?"

"I'm a fitness trainer. Weights are my forte."

"Get out of here," he said in disbelief. She was too small to lift anything heavier than her son.

"Want to arm wrestle?"

So that explained how she'd body-slammed him that night in the hospital. Concussion and all, he remembered that.

"After the way you demolished me in darts, I think I should pass." But the chance to touch her was tempting. He wouldn't mind finding out if she was as toned and tight everywhere else.

"You're a bigger coward than the junior high boys in my Sunday school class. At least they'll try me."

A Sunday school teacher. He liked that. Maybe she could teach him some new tunes. "Any of them ever win?"

"Now and then."

"When you let them?"

She smiled and he knew he was right. Fascinating woman. "What got you interested in fitness?"

A cloud came and went on her face, making him wonder. What secrets did Becka-Rebecka hide?

Pouring two glasses of Cookie's lemonade, she

handed one to Jett before settling into the chair across from his. "I've always liked sports."

A woman who actually liked sports. Sweet. She was full of surprises tonight, and the more she sprang on him, the more intrigued he became. "Any in particular?"

With a little laugh, she swigged her lemonade, ran a tempting tongue over her lips and said, "All of them. Everything, especially if they involved water. Then I discovered that some games are too dangerous to play so I chose bodybuilding."

"A control sport." Which didn't surprise him at all, given the way she kept a tight rein on herself, her son, even him when she could.

"And very safe. With a son to raise safety became my most important consideration."

"Where's the thrill in life without a little danger?"

"Life doesn't have to be a thrill, Jett."

"It does to me."

"Why?"

Now, there was fine question he'd asked himself a dozen times. "When I was a kid, I liked scaring my mother. After a while, I enjoyed the excitement too much to stop."

She turned incredulous brown eyes his way. "You liked scaring your poor mother?"

He shrugged and stared down at the lemon slice floating in his glass. How did he tell anyone that pulling dangerous stunts was the only way he ever got his mother's attention? Attention that only lasted for a few minutes of admonishment before she returned to her latest personal crisis. "Mom had other things on her mind besides me and my siblings."

"What could be more important than her child's safety?"

He'd wondered that himself a few times before deciding he must not be all that important. "Let's say my mother isn't a cookie-baking kind of mom. She and her husbands had other agendas."

"Husbands, as in several?" He didn't mind the question. She sounded interested but not judgmental. Besides, he'd long ago accepted his parents and their significant others for who they were, and the knowledge had reaffirmed his conclusion that marriage meant divorce and a lifetime of trouble.

"Four at last count, though she married my father twice—as punishment, I think." He swallowed a hefty drink of the tart lemonade, backhanded his mouth and grinned. "Can we dance now?"

She crossed her legs and leaned back into the chair. "You lost, remember?"

Touching his temple, Jett faked a frown. "I think my concussion's acting up again. Didn't you promise to dance with me as consolation if I lost the dart game?"

"Ha-ha." She checked the machine, still rhythmically working his knee in and out. "How's the leg doing?"

"So far, so good."

"How's the pain, on a scale of one to ten?"

"Three."

"Most people would probably call that a six."

"I'm not most people." He grabbed her hand and pulled her toward him. "But I am a dancing fool."

"Don't, Jett." She stiffened like starched underwear, pulled away and began straightening his bedroom as though she'd been the one to toss his towels and magazines on the floor. "Dylan should be here soon, and we still have plenty of work to do on that knee."

Running away again, he thought, the way she did every time she started to enjoy herself.

By the time Kati arrived with Dylan, Becka was getting antsy. They were fifteen minutes late, and she'd begun to fear something terrible had happened to her son. Even Jett's teasing and joking hadn't helped take her mind off the fear.

"Dylan!" The second he burst through the door she went down on her knees in front of him. "Slow down. You'll fall."

He put on the brakes, his smile falling away. He stuck his thumb in his mouth.

Kati, with her son, Evan, in tow, followed him in. "He's excited, Becka. Ask him to tell you his news."

But Becka could only think of his safety. "I thought something had happened to the three of you."

Kati rested one hand on the swell of her pregnant belly. "Michelle Martin was late again and we couldn't lock up until she picked up her kids."

Such a simple answer. Why hadn't she thought that? Why did the fear always come first and common sense after?

"Hey, Dylan. Hi, Evan." Jett drew the attention back to the children. "You two hombres come here and give me a high-five."

Evan launched himself at his uncle and was caught in midair before doing any damage to the knee. Dylan squirmed out of Becka's tight hug, moving slower, but with every bit as much eagerness toward Jett. Becka was amazed and distressed at the amount of attention Dylan wanted from the cowboy. During the week they'd been coming here, Dylan hung on to Jett's every word, climbed on his lap and pestered him with his childish questions. She supposed it was her son's lack of a father that made him crave a man's attention. To his credit, Jett showed enormous patience and warmth for her child.

Given Jett's lifestyle Becka wasn't sure if she approved but was comforted by the knowledge that the acquaintance was temporary. They wouldn't be around the risk-taking cowboy long enough for her son to be influenced.

"Come on now, Evan," Kati said, holding out a hand. "Let's go see Daddy."

Evan leaped from his uncle's lap and rocketed out the door with his mom.

"That boy has energy enough for two," Becka said.

"He's a normal boy, Becka. Energy is part of the package."

Was he criticizing because Dylan was quiet and timid and still sucked his thumb? "I don't want Dylan behaving so rambunctiously. He'll get hurt."

"Getting hurt is part of the package, too. Little boys are made of strong stuff. Wounds heal."

She wanted to tell him that some wounds don't heal, but that was a subject she wouldn't broach with a wild man like Jett. Instead she turned her attention to her son.

"How was your day today, baby?"

Dylan ignored her, reaching his arms up toward Jett instead. A twinge of jealousy, quickly squelched, pinched her. How foolish to be jealous of Dylan's need for a male role model.

Jett pulled Dylan onto his lap and brushed the dark hair back from the child's forehead. "Hey there, ace, what's up?"

"I spelled my name. All by myself."

Jett clapped him gently on the back. "Sweet deal, Lucille."

Dylan giggled. "Not Lucille. Dylan."

"Get us a paper and pencil, Becka-Rebecka. This boy has some showing off to do."

So this was the news Dylan had been so excited about. With a catch beneath her rib cage, Becka rummaged around on Jett's desk, came up with writing materials and handed them to the two males. Her baby was growing up too fast.

"All right, boy, do your stuff." Jett positioned the paper on the arm of his chair so Dylan could lean across his lap to write. With painstaking effort and his tongue between his teeth, Dylan drew the letters of his name then straightened with a triumphant grin.

"See?" He held the paper toward the two adults. Crooked letters of varying size sprawled over the sheet. Becka had never seen such beautiful penmanship.

"That is awesome, son." She grabbed his face and kissed him loudly.

"Hey, I can write my name, too," Jett teased.

And while Becka made a face at the joke, Dylan pushed the paper toward Jett and said, "Let's see."

The adults locked eyes and laughed. Then Jett obliged, writing his name in neat print below Dylan's. "Not as good as yours," he said, "but not bad. Mind if I keep this?"

"Okay," Dylan said, and Becka felt a wave of disappointment. She'd wanted that for herself.

"Becka-Rebecka, will you get some tape and hang this on my door so I can see it all the time?"

Dylan beamed and Becka appreciated Jett's kindness, even if he was making it harder for her and Dylan to maintain a safe distance. She didn't want to see him as a decent man, couldn't afford to. His lifestyle spoke volumes about the kind of man he really was.

"Mama puts my drawlings on the 'fridgerator."

"Just where they belong, too, but since I don't have a 'fridgerator, the door will have to do." Jett held the paper out to Becka, then motioned toward the plate of muffins. "Want some lemonade and a muffin?"

"I wanna go play with Evan." Dylan sent Becka a hopeful look.

"No, baby," she said. "You can sit here and watch TV while Jett and I finish up."

"I tired of TV. I wanna play with Evan. He gots toys."

As much as she hated disappointing her child, Becka refused. She wanted him here close so she could watch him. She saw Jett's lips tighten in disapproval, but ignored him. What did he, of all people, know about raising a child in a world wrought with dangers?

By eight o'clock, Dylan was sitting in the big blue chair like a thumb-sucking robot, and Jett was wishing he had a little more time alone with Becka-Rebecka.

His knee throbbed like a son of a gun as it always did after she tortured and nagged him for four hours, but he still hated to see her leave. She was fun, though she tried hard not to be. Tonight he'd broken through that crust of ice and gotten her talking, found out some things about her life and he'd been pretty pleased with himself a few times when she'd laughed or flirted in response to something he said.

Things were definitely looking up. But as far as he was concerned, they'd still done too much work and not enough play.

Becka cut through his thoughts. "Do you think you can work this PT machine by yourself tomorrow?"

He looked up in horror. "You're not quitting, are you?" Not now. Not when she was about to be his. Well, maybe things weren't that good yet, but they would be.

"No, silly. But if you'll do the time on the machine alone, we'll have more time to work on the exercise regimen when I'm here."

He groaned. "Do we have to?"

She stuck a hand on that perfectly formed hip of hers. "Do you want to ride bulls again?"

Other than seduce his nurse, riding bulls again was about the only thing Jett did want to do right now. And Becka knew it. "You don't play fair."

"Nursing 101, never let the patient gain the upper hand."

"Okay, I'll do the machine myself, if I can, and let you torture me longer tomorrow." He shot her an ornery grin. "I know other forms of torture that are so much more fun. Couldn't I teach you some of those?"

She didn't honor that with an answer. Instead she gathered her belongings and reached a hand toward Dylan. "Time to go, baby."

The little boy, looking bored out of his mind, gave an exaggerated sigh of relief and slid out of the chair.

Jett felt for the kid. Why didn't she let him play and run and act like a boy?

"Bye, ace. See you tomorrow. Thanks for letting me keep your paper."

As soon as Becka closed the door, Jett shoved up from his chair and hobbled to the window. He'd no more than pulled aside the curtain than he asked himself what was going on. Why was he standing here watching his nurse walk to her car? And why did he feel this inexplicable sense of loneliness as soon as she left?

Boredom. Confinement. That had to be it.

The setting August sun gleamed off Becka's red hair as she opened the car door, reached in the back seat and extracted a large plastic water container. Dylan stood patiently, sucking his thumb.

Colt had told him about putting water in Becka's car one time. Did she do that every night?

Without giving a thought to his knee, Jett turned and headed outside.

As soon as Becka spotted him, she set the water container down in front of the car and shouted, "What are you doing? You shouldn't be out here on that leg. No weight-bearing whatsoever. Remember?"

With more effort than he wanted to admit, he limped to the front of her car and fought against leaning on the hood.

"The better question is what are you doing?" He pointed to the container and the opened hood. "Is your car in that bad a condition?"

She stiffened. "It only needs water and we'll be fine."

She tried to move past him but he blocked her with

his body and frowned down at the inner workings of an ancient vehicle. The tub didn't look so healthy.

Removing the radiator cap, he peered into the hole, then shook his head in disgust. Balancing as much as possible on his good leg, he lifted the water container and filled the radiator. The car glub-glubbed most of the contents.

"Cell phones don't work well out here, you know," he told her, frowning. "If you get stranded, you're at anybody's mercy."

"I don't have a cell phone, anyway."

"Why not?" Everyone needed a cell phone, especially a woman alone—and he didn't care how chauvinistic that sounded.

"They cost money. So do cars."

So money, not his charm and good looks, had been her motivation for taking this job. A guy could get a complex.

He slammed the hood, noticed the dent in the front, but kept his mouth shut. The car alone should have been a major clue that she was hard up for cash. The heap was ancient and in lousy condition—not safe at all for a woman and child to be traveling in. If she was his woman...

"Why don't you drive my truck? Leave your car here." Where had that come from? Nobody drove his truck except him. But he found he liked thinking of Becka behind the wheel, safe inside his new Dodge Ram instead of in this death trap.

Becka looked as surprised as he felt. "Thanks, but I don't think so."

He'd sleep better knowing she and Dylan were safe. "I'm not using it."

She smiled and crossed her arms. "And neither am I."

He grinned. Darn, but she was cute. The sprinkle of freckles across her nose beckoned him. Holding to the fender, he moved toward her. With each step, she backed up a little more until he had her right where he wanted her—against the side of the car.

Her golden eyes widened and he was sure this time they widened from anticipation. Sparks sizzled in the air between them that didn't have a thing to do with the blazing summer sun. She might play cool and distant, but a fire burned beneath those pink scrubs.

Bracing a hand on each side of her face, he said softly, "Take my truck."

Her luscious mouth moved, sending his gut into a clench. "No."

She made no effort to escape him, only stood there, gazing up at him with that light in her eyes. The thought occurred to him that she was flirting; playing, just as he was, and that they were no longer discussing his vehicle.

"Take it," he whispered and moved a little closer.

"Too risky," she murmured, refusing his offer of more than the truck.

"You want to."

"No."

"Liar." He slid one finger over her charming freckles, down her nose, over the soft, moist lips, and down the warm column of her throat. Her felt her swallow, then the thud-thud of her pulse. His own answered and the adrenaline rush he craved kicked into high gear.

Sweet. He leaned in, eager to ignite the embers smoldering inside Becka-Rebecka.

Suddenly she pushed at him, sending him hopping backward on one leg.

"Dylan," she screamed.

Quick as lightning even with the bad knee, Jett whirled to look for the boy. In his preoccupation with the mother, he'd forgotten all about the child.

It didn't take long to locate him. Not twenty yards away, Dylan had climbed the rail fence of the corral, looking perfectly unharmed.

Jett reached for Becka's arm. She was trembling. "Hey. He's okay."

But she paid him no mind. "Dylan," she yelled, "get away from there *right* now."

The boy's shoulders slumped as he climbed down and started slowly back toward the car.

"Becka, I said he's fine. Leave the kid alone for once. Nothing over there can hurt him. There aren't even any animals around, and if there were, he would still be fine. Calm down."

Spinning toward him, she poked a finger in his chest. "Don't tell me to calm down. He's my son. I'm responsible for him. I won't have him turned into some reckless risk taker hell-bent on killing himself for a thrill."

Was she referring to him, just because he liked a little adventure? That got his dander up. "No, you're turning him into a wuss instead."

"How dare you criticize me. You have no idea—" She stopped, pressed her fingers to her mouth and looked ready to cry.

Oh, man. He threw his hands into the air.

"All right. Hey. He's your kid. Make him a sissy if you choose. Why should I care?"

Turning with as much dignity as he could muster considering the metal cage around his knee and the shock of pain pulsing up his leg, he limped back toward the house. Why was he so bugged by the way she coddled the boy, smothering all the fire out of him?

Neither Dylan nor Becka was his responsibility—heaven forbid—so why did he bother? Why did he care at all?

The question haunted him all the rest of the evening.

Chapter Five

The next day was Becka's Saturday off from the hospital, though for all she accomplished she would have been better off working. Jett Garrett, with his seductive blue eyes and pent-up energy, tormented her thoughts all day.

Tossing the final load of clothes into the dryer, she added a softener sheet and pushed *Start*.

She still couldn't believe her behavior last night. She'd let her defenses down again, going with the pull of attraction, the rush of excitement, and had almost let something terrible happen to her son.

Hadn't she learned her lesson with Chris—that one moment out of control could destroy everything?

Yet when Jett had limped away in anger, she'd longed to call him back and apologize. But apologize for what? She'd only been protecting her child.

Taking the basket of warm, clean clothes into the living room, she sat on the couch and began folding Dylan's T-shirts.

"I need more tape, Mommy." Along with an empty roll of Scotch tape, Dylan held up yet another sheet of paper bearing his name.

Since climbing out of bed that morning Dylan had entertained himself with pen and paper. Employing long strips of tape, he'd decorated the refrigerator and was now working on covering the front door with evidence of his new skill.

Becka smiled at the adorably crooked letters. "Sorry, baby, that's the only roll. We'll stop by Wal-Mart on our way to the Garretts' and pick up a new one."

Although, in truth, she wished she didn't have to go to the Garretts' today. Yesterday had proven just how dangerous Jett was to her sense of control.

And to make matters worse, she liked the guy. He was funny and warm and yes, sexy. In those moments when he had pressed her against the warm metal of her old Fairlane, insisting she drive his truck instead of her dilapidated old car, her heart had nearly come out of her chest. He'd wanted to kiss her. And she'd wanted him to. And if that wasn't bad enough, the throw-caution-to-the-wind daredevil who didn't even protect himself had made her feel protected and cared for when he insisted she take his truck.

Jett Garrett confused her almost as much as he scared her.

"Stupid, stupid," she muttered viciously slamming a pair of shorts onto a stack.

Dylan looked up from the coffee table, a worried frown between his brown eyes. "Me, Mommy?"

Instantly sorry for the outburst, Becka stroked a hand over his dark hair. "No, baby, not you. Mommy."

He studied her for a moment, then climbed up on the couch and wrapped his arms around her. His heated little-boy scent mingled with the smell of clean laundry. Heart clenching with love for her only child, she smothered him in a playful bear hug.

Infectious giggle filling the room, he was struggling to escape when someone knocked on the door. With a final smooch on the forehead, Becka set Dylan free and went to the door.

"Hi, Sherm." Sherman Benchley, her insurance man and occasional date, stood on the porch, sun gleaming off his perfectly groomed blond hair. Unlatching the storm door, she pushed it open, beckoning him inside. A waft of hot air rushed into the living room where a window unit struggled to cool the interior.

Dressed in his usual suit and tie in spite of the August heat, Sherman stepped in on her faded blue carpet.

"What brings you by this afternoon?"

"I happened to be in the neighborhood. Mitch Hasworth wrecked his truck yesterday." He held up one manicured hand. "Nothing serious. A fender-bender at the corner of Robinson and Starling. But he'd asked me to stop by and have a look."

"I'm glad Mitch is okay." Wishing her pile of underwear was somewhere other than the coffee table, she motioned toward the couch. "Have a seat, Sherman. I'll get you a glass of ice water."

Anyone else she would have offered tea or soda, but Sherman's stomach gave him problems.

"Yes, the weather's certainly warm today." Careful

not to wrinkle his pleated slacks, Sherm eased onto the sofa, crossing one knee precisely over the other. A pair of brown wing-tips gleamed in the light.

Becka got the water for him then perched on the edge of the chair. Sherm. He was so uncomplicated. Not at all like Jett. She glanced at the clock. If she was going by Wal-Mart, she needed to leave soon.

"I don't mean to be rude, Sherman, but I have to make a home visit soon."

"Is that what's been keeping you occupied lately? I've tried to call you twice this week and found no one at home." He sipped at the water.

"That's it exactly. You know how much I need the extra money."

Sherman's company had held the policy on Chris's wave runner—a policy that paid off the expensive water toy but paid nothing on medical and funeral expenses. Whether because of compassion or attraction, Sherm had taken her, a pregnant young widow under his wing, helping her arrange bank loans and payment schedules to satisfy her debtors. She didn't know how she would have managed without good old Sherm. She owed him big-time.

Dylan, who'd been happily drawing his name on yet another sheet of paper, sidled up to Sherman. "I can write my name."

Sherman gave the boy a cursory glance. "Very nice." Then turned back to Becka. "I was planning to come over Monday evening. That's mother's Bunco game night, you know. I thought we could watch a video. Will you be working then, too?"

Becka's attention ping-ponged from Sherman to her

son. Dylan stood beside the insurance man, the paper hanging from one hand at his side, sucking his thumb. Her heart went out to her little boy. He was so proud of that name and Sherman had hardly acknowledged the accomplishment.

The image of Dylan on Jett's lap flashed behind her eyes. Jett, the careless one, had cared enough to notice. The idea annoyed her, both at Sherman and at Jett. Dylan needed a sensible, calm man as a roll model, not a maniac like Jett.

Becka rose. "I don't know yet, Sherman. Let me call you later when I have my schedule better organized."

Sherman took the hint and rose with her, going to the door. As they stepped out onto the wooden porch, a silver and blue pickup truck careened around the corner and screeched to a halt on the street in front of her house.

Becka's stomach flip-flopped. Jett. What on earth…?

She was off the porch and across the dry, crackling grass in nothing flat. He had no business being out and about on that leg. Never mind the leap of energy shooting through her veins. She was concerned for his medical condition and nothing else.

As she approached the truck, Jett shoved the door open and stretched out both arms as if he expected her to jump into them. Pulse quickening, she stopped dead still and worked for control.

Dylan came flying past, catapulted into Jett's arms and was pulled inside the truck. Becka felt like an idiot.

"I thought you were mad at us," the child said, pressing one hand to each of Jett's freshly shaved cheeks.

"Mad?" Jett drew back in mock horror. "I'd never be mad at you, Dylan. You're my bud."

"What about Mommy?" Dylan cast an anxious glance at Becka that made her chest tighten. She hadn't realized the tension between her and Jett would worry Dylan.

Jett shot her a naughty wink. "I'm not mad at her, either."

"Okay." Satisfied, Dylan climbed across Jett's lap, settling into the passenger's seat. "Let's go."

Jett laughed. "Where?"

"Wal-Mart."

Jett squinted at Becka, blue eyes twinkling. "Are we headed to Wal-Mart?"

The magnetism of his larger-than-life personality pulled at her. Resisting with everything she had, Becka placed both hands on her hipbones and asked, "What are you doing here?"

Wearing a half grin, Jett looked from her to Sherman. "Interrupting something, it looks like."

Good heavens, she'd forgotten all about her guest. Sherman stood next to her, expression stiff and curious. Tiny beads of moisture glistened on his forehead.

"This is my friend, Sherman Benchley. Sherman, meet Jett Garrett, my patient, who should be at home, taking care of himself." Sherman leaned into the truck to shake hands, but neither man smiled.

Sherman, usually so civil and always on the lookout for a new customer gazed at the immobilizer encasing Jett's knee and said curtly, "I trust you had sufficient insurance coverage." Then he turned his attention to Becka. "Call me."

Moving stiffly, which wasn't all that unusual for Sherman, he got into his Oldsmobile and drove away.

"I don't think Mr. Bentley liked me." Jett grinned a grin that said he didn't care a bit. His left leg poked straight out in front of him, the metal cage barely fitting beneath the dashboard. Only the luxury of a clutchless automatic transmission made it possible for him to be behind the steering wheel in the first place.

"Benchley. And he's a very nice man."

"Is he your type?" At her questioning look he went on, reminding her of their conversation the night before. "Safe. Predictable. *Boring.* Weren't those the qualities you want in a man?"

Those were exactly the qualities she desired, right down to the boring part. Sherm didn't make her pulse race or her blood hot, but that was well and good. She'd had enough adrenaline highs with Chris to last a lifetime.

"If you're asking if Sherman and I are dating, the answer is yes. We see each other now and then. Now, stop avoiding my question. What are you doing here?"

"You wouldn't drive my truck, so my truck came to pick you up."

"That wasn't necessary." Nice, but not necessary. The considerate gesture sent a shaft of warmth through her insides. Jett wasn't supposed to be considerate. A man like him only thought of himself, but from the moment he'd arrived and taken Dylan into his arms, her insides had behaved in a ridiculous manner.

"That old tub of yours is on its last legs. It can't take the wear and tear between here and my place. You're going to get stranded."

"How did you know where I live?"

"Rattlesnake Municipal. I stopped there first." He

pinned her with a mock scowl. "Why didn't you tell me you were off work today?"

"We weren't exactly exchanging pleasantries when I left last night."

"True. But if I'd known, I could have come earlier and taken you and Dylan to the dune buggy races over on Cooper's Hill."

Once Becka had loved racing her own dune buggy, but there was no way she'd let Jett in on that secret. Those days of recklessness were over for good.

She decided to ignore his assumption that she would have gone anywhere with him and instead attacked the obvious problem. His lack of common sense about his own health drove her nuts. Irresponsible, that's what he was. Just like Chris.

"You've been walking around on that leg."

"Nope. I sprouted wings and flew—after sitting in the torture machine for my prescribed six hours."

He shuddered and Becka suffered a twinge of compassion. Confinement of that sort drove anyone to distraction, but especially an energetic live wire like Jett. Still, he could undo all the good they'd done by putting weight on the still-healing knee.

"Jett, I talked to the orthopod earlier today to update the PT orders. He says if you reinjure that knee in any way…"

"Don't nag, Becka-Rebecka. I know all that. One false move and I'm a candidate for a rocking chair instead of a buckin' bull. I'll do better, I promise." He reached out and snagged her hand, shaking her arm up and down in a teasing manner. "Come on, don't be mad anymore. I'm going insane stuck out there all day."

So that was why he'd come into town. Not because

he worried over her car, but out of boredom. She should have known.

"Let me take you and Dylan to an early dinner before we head to the ranch."

"Pizza!" Dylan shouted from beneath Jett's right arm.

Jett scrubbed a hand across her son's hair. "Works for me. How about you, Becka-Rebecka? Will you have pizza with us men?"

Struck by the enormous desire to do exactly that and by the bigger fear of getting too close, she shook her head. "I don't think so, Jett. Let Dylan out of there and we'll be out at the ranch at the appointed time."

"I wanna go with Jett." Dylan rose up on his knees and beamed a pleading look in her direction. "Pizza, Mom."

Pizza was a rare treat on her budget, and like all kids, Dylan loved the stuff. So did she.

"Come on, Mom," Jett said with a sexy grin that curled her toes into the crispy grass. "Don't deny the boy a hot, cheesy pizza."

She felt herself relenting. "Using my son that way is not playing fair."

"Never said I play fair." He pumped his dark eyebrows. "But I do play. And I play to win."

Which was exactly Becka's concern.

Searching for a way out, she said. "I have to change into my uniform."

Laser-blue eyes shifted over her shorts and tank top. How was it possible that a single look could cause her to tingle everywhere? "No need to change. You're working for me. And I don't have a problem with what you're wearing."

She had a problem with what she was wearing. Jett

stirred up enough trouble without her letting down her professional guard.

"Give me five minutes."

"And you'll let me buy you pizza?"

She had to eat. What possible harm could there be in stopping for a meal of pizza? Jett couldn't do anything crazy or dangerous in a public restaurant. She and Dylan would be perfectly safe.

"I'm driving my car," she said as she walked away. Behind her, Jett laughed.

"Well, look at this. If it ain't joyridin' Jett himself." Above throbbing music and the *ching-ching* of video games, the dark-haired manager of the Pizza Palace cocked a finger and thumb in Jett's direction the minute he hobbled through the door. Her flirtatious smile was not lost on Becka. "Taken any rides in borrowed cars lately?"

Much to Becka's disgust Jett laughed and flirted right back. "Better hush that stuff, Barbie. I don't want everybody to know about my wicked teenage days."

"You can't fool me, Jett Garrett. You haven't changed. I heard you was holed up out at your ranch with a bum leg from some of your wild adventures. And I see the rumor was true." She nodded toward the pair of crutches riding beneath his armpits.

Becka was still amazed he'd remembered to bring them with him. She hadn't expected him to show that much common sense.

"Totally innocent explanation. I stumbled while pickin' daisies in my grandma's garden."

Barbie chortled. "So you still plan on making the NFR this year?"

"Yep. Nothing can stop me."

Barbie's doubtful look took in Jett's handicapped condition. "Not even that metal rod sticking out the side of your knee?"

Jett hitched his chin toward Becka. "That's where Becka comes in. She's my nurse and personal slave driver. She'll have me fixed up and on the road in no time." He looked from one woman to the other. "You two know each other, don't you?"

"Sure." Barbie leaned an elbow on the counter. "Becka was the nurse on duty when my Randy got dog bit earlier this summer. She made a bad situation easier to tolerate."

Becka saw lots of dog bites but Randy's was particularly nasty. "How's Randy doing?"

"Oh, he's out terrorizing the neighborhood again like any self-respecting ten-year-old. Just a little bitty scar to remind him not to tease a rottweiler. But I'll never forget how you calmed him down and helped him get through the needles and stitches. You're a good nurse."

While the women chitchatted, Jett swung around to the other side of the counter, found a paper hat, then came back to where Dylan stood holding Becka's hand.

"Here ya go, ace. Your own pizza maker's hat." He slipped the tricornered, brown-and-red hat over the boy's dark hair. "Now that you're official, I'll bet Miss Barbara will let you make your own pizza." He flashed a stunning smile in the manager's direction. "How about it, Barbie? Me and my best bud decorating our own pizza?"

With a grinning shrug, Barbie made a come-on gesture with her hand. "The evening rush is still an hour away. Come around here and I'll show you how to get started."

As Dylan moved around the counter, one hand resting in Jett's, a surge of anxiety charged through Becka's chest. "No!"

At the sharp cry, heard clearly over the thump of hip-hop music, the other two adults turned to stare. Dylan stuck his thumb in his mouth.

Embarrassment rose in Becka's cheeks as she noticed that the half-dozen customers also stared in her direction. "I'd rather Dylan not be near the stove. He could get burned."

"Chill out, Becka-Rebecka," Jett said gently. He draped an arm around Dylan's sturdy shoulders, snugging him close. "I'm right here. I won't let anything happen to the boy."

Yeah, like she trusted joy-riding Jett with her baby.

Becka crossed her arms. "I don't think so."

Wearing a funny smile she didn't begin to understand, Jett leaned the crutches against the wall, then hobbled around the counter and pulled at her arms, effectively uncrossing them as his hands slid down to grasp hers.

His voice went soft, personal. "Come on," he coaxed. "Help us make pizza. It'll be fun."

He might as well have been asking her to leap into a bonfire. Every moment spent in Jett's company eroded her control, made her want to do things she shouldn't. Dangerous things. Hadn't he already convinced her to ride in his truck when she'd had every intention of driving her own car?

"Pease, Mommy." Dylan's brown eyes looked up at

her with longing, then at Jett with a kind of desperate hope. Her resistance took a serious hit.

The man had asked to make pizza, not love. Why was she making such a big deal out of it? She was right here, watching Dylan every second. She could make certain he was safe.

Jett tugged at her hands. "It's only pizza, Becka. A few sprinkles of cheese, some pepperoni."

The fragrance of hot, spicy pizza had her stomach growling.

Suddenly despising the ever-present fear and her tendency to overreact, she gave Jett her fiercest look. "No anchovies?"

The corners of his eyes crinkled with laughter—and the hint of victory. "My word of honor. No anchovies. Right, Dylan?"

"Right." The fact that Dylan didn't know an anchovy from an ankle bracelet made Becka laugh. At least, she hoped it was Dylan's sweet innocence and not the zing of exhilaration she experienced at doing something as mundane as creating a pizza with Jett Garrett.

"Okay. And then we *must* get moving. That knee won't exercise itself."

Jett groaned. "And I thought pizza would distract you from your evil mission."

Rolling her eyes to keep from grinning, Becka followed Jett behind the counter. Barbie, still flirting with Jett while welcoming Becka and Dylan, placed the prepared pan of dough on the counter and showed all three the containers of toppings.

"Stand on this, little fella," she said to Dylan as she

scooted a low footstool up to the counter. The child clambered up and stood staring in fascination at the wide array of toppings.

"Which ones do you like, Dylan?" Jett asked, and Becka noticed him leaning most of his weight against the counter. Guilt suffused her. Jett had no business up on that leg, and as his nurse she was responsible to see that he followed doctor's orders. But instead she was behaving like a starstruck teenager, letting him talk her into doing something detrimental.

"Jett, you need to either sit down or get back on those crutches."

"In a minute. Dylan has a pizza to make first."

The child dipped a freshly washed and dried hand into a small bowl and began to sprinkle cheese onto the pizza. Bits of mozzarella scattered along the counter and fell to the floor.

Becka started toward him. "He's making a mess."

Jett stopped her with a hand on her arm. "Let him do it. Messes can be cleaned up."

"He might fall."

"Not a chance." Grabbing one crutch which he jammed beneath his arm, Jett moved behind Dylan. The boy looked up, adoration in his expression.

"I like cheese."

"Me too, bud."

"Here." Dylan shoved the bowl toward his new hero. "Let's share."

Becka watched with a catch in her throat as joyriding Jett and her baby made an awful mess and created an absolutely wonderful pizza.

"Mommy likes olives."

Jett motioned to the bowl. "Here, Mommy, put some on. Let's make a pizza-man face."

For several delicious minutes, Becka was pressed next to Jett's hard, heated side, feeling young and carefree while the three of them created a face with olive eyes, a pepperoni nose and tomato lips. A man, a woman and a child—almost like a family. The sudden longing for something more than work and worry pulled at Becka. Foolish, senseless thoughts, given the dangerous company she was keeping.

Dylan's childish laugh resounded through the restaurant and she let his joy erase her longing. Dylan was her life. And if she ever needed or wanted a man in her life, Sherman was available. Jett was her patient. A troublesome, frightening patient whose reckless ways could easily rub off on Dylan—and her. But not to worry. Soon she'd collect her paychecks and be rid of him forever.

And now that she'd decided as much, she could relax and have a few minutes of harmless fun.

Chapter Six

Knee trapped in the shark machine, Jett lay in his recliner doing arm curls with the dumbbells Becka had brought him. Bull-riding videos played across the TV screen, but his mind wasn't on studying the bucking tendencies of rodeo bulls or on maintaining the upper body strength necessary to stay on one. His mind was on a tiny red-haired nurse who brought out the protective instincts in him.

He sighed in disgust and banged the remote against the chair arm.

The woman could body-slam a sumo wrestler. She could take care of herself. Besides, he wasn't the type to go worrying about a woman.

So what was the deal here? Why couldn't he stop thinking about that hunk of rusted, overheating metal of hers? And why couldn't he stop thinking about how bald the tires were? Or about how cute she looked with pizza cheese clinging to her red hair.

Tonight she was driving his truck back into Rattlesnake even if he had to let all the air out of her tires. If sweet talk wouldn't do it a little bribery would.

"Cookie!" he yelled.

When the cook didn't appear, he put down one of the dumbbells, fumbled around on the floor, found a shoe and chunked it against the door.

In seconds, the door slammed backward, reverberating off the wall. "What in tarnation are you bellering about?"

Jett winced at Cookie's foghorn voice. "You're the one bellowing."

"I was making an apple pie for Miss Kati." Flour dusted the apron covering the old man's forty-pound paunch. Jett caught a whiff of cinnamon.

"Kati still has you wrapped around her finger, huh?"

Cookie sniffed. "Miss Kati is expecting a baby, in case you hadn't noticed. Pregnant ladies get to eat whatever they want. And she wants one of my apple pies."

"Is there enough for company?"

Cookie slammed a pair of beefy fists onto equally beefy hips. "If you're inviting that Melissa girl, there ain't enough."

"What if it's not Melissa?"

"I got my hands full feeding that bunch of hay-haulers. I ain't cooking for none of your buckle bunnies."

Jett wished with all his heart Becka was a rodeo groupie. It would sure simplify things. "I was thinking of asking Becka and Dylan to eat supper with us tonight."

Not that she meant anything to him. Heck no, but he

was bored stupid, the only reasonable explanation for his sudden case of worryitis.

Cookie's eyes lit up. "Well, now, if that ain't a miracle, I don't know what one is. Maybe that bull done you a favor by tossing you on your head."

Jett shifted uncomfortably. His knee reacted with a stab of pain. "Don't go getting funny ideas. I invite lots of women to supper. Lots of *different* women. But Becka and Dylan are already here. They may as well eat."

"Little thing could use some fatting up."

Jett wanted to say he thought Becka's body was perfect, but Cookie would jump on that like a rat on a Cheez-It.

"She works pretty hard." Sometimes he wondered how she fit everything in. "Even when she's here she never lets up." He laughed shortly. "Some days I wish she would. She works me as hard as she works herself."

"I've noticed as much. Not that a little honest work would hurt you." Cookie bustled over to the desk and with a disgusted huff tossed the empty tortilla chip wrappers into the trash can. "Two jobs and a young 'un would keep anybody skinny."

"She helps her dad a lot, too. Health problems, she said. And from the looks of that old rattletrap I'd say money is an issue, wouldn't you?" He didn't know why that bugged him. Dylan, he supposed. He didn't want the little guy doing without things.

"I 'spect money's tight. Why else would she drive out here and put up with a lazy no-account like you?"

Jett frowned, the worryitis returning. His desk clock read three-thirty. Becka was on the road in that death trap.

He hated to worry. He never worried. But he kept seeing those bald tires.

What was wrong with him lately? Too many pain pills? Nah, couldn't be that. He hadn't taken any. Must be those uninvited guests—the sharks in his knee. They were enough to turn a man into a complete wuss.

"If you're gonna stand around in here and insult me," he said to Cookie, "make yourself useful. Change that video to the one marked Sinsation. I'm gonna ride that ornery bull next go-round."

"You Garretts ain't got a lick of sense." As he switched out the video, Cookie shook his head, setting in motion the blackjack sprouts that substituted for hair. "You'd be better off forgettin' about them bulls, find you a good woman and stick around here to help your brother. He's got his hands full trying to run this ranch while *you* run all over the country chasing women and trying to get yourself killed."

Jett made a face. "Castrating bulls isn't as much fun as it used to be."

"There's plenty more to do around here than that. Colt spends hours every night worrying over the books. You got a head for figgers—and I ain't just talking about the female kind."

"Colt doesn't need my help." They'd agreed from the outset that Colt would run the ranch his way while Jett shared expenses and profits. "The ranch is a great place to heal, but you know me, Cookie. I don't like staying in one place very long."

"Don't you feel any kind of responsibility to this place other than whirling in like a tornado and whirling out whenever the mood suits you? Don't you think Colt would like more time with his wife and babies? Even with the ranch hands we got working for us, he never gets any time off."

Jett hated when Cookie got on a soapbox, but he hadn't considered how hard the ranch might be on Colt now that he was a family man. "Why not?"

"Ah, that brother of yours thinks he's the only one who can run the place."

"See? There's your answer. He wouldn't want me interfering." Not that he'd mind doing something useful while he was here. Anything to pass the time.

"The ranch don't belong to the hired hands, but it does belong to you."

He'd always figured if Colt didn't like the ranch work, he wouldn't do it. That's the way they both lived their lives. They went where they wanted, did what they wanted whenever they chose. Or they had until Kati came along. Now he wasn't so sure.

"I'll talk to Colt. But don't expect much." He didn't want to be here permanently. Three weeks was about to make him a candidate for one of those talk show psychiatrists. "I have places to go, things to do. Wouldn't want to disappoint all those single ladies."

Cookie pushed a button, paused a bull in midbuck, slapped the remote on Jett's chair arm, and moved to the open doorway. He turned and nailed Jett with a stare. "You don't need to go nowhere to find a single lady. You got one coming out here every night. And unless I miss my guess, you're hankering for her and too big a fool to admit it. You may have metal in your leg, but quit acting like you got rocks in your head to go with it."

Jett chunked the remote at the grinning face but

missed a mile as the cagey old cook chuckled off down the hallway.

He was not sticking around. No way. He was too close to the finals to throw in the towel now. Nothing was going to stop him. Not a bad knee. Not this ranch. And certainly not a woman.

Becka, weary from a busy day at the hospital, rubbed the back of her neck as the Garretts' portly cook/house-keeper let her into the house.

"Hi, Cookie." Stepping into the cool oak hallway, she took a deep cleansing breath. She'd only worked out a few times since taking this job, and the lack of regular exercise had taken a toll in fatigue and muscle tension. Tonight she'd brought enough equipment to change that.

"You look tuckered."

"Thanks," she said, grinning wryly.

The old cook chortled. "Oh, you're still perty as a pitcher. But you need a good supper and some apple pie. You do like apple pie, don't you? It's my specialty."

"Everyone likes apple pie."

"Good. I've set a place for you and that the young 'un. Supper's at six."

Becka blinked in confusion. Normally she brought a sandwich for Dylan and didn't worry about eating until she returned home. Had she just accepted a dinner invitation?

But before she had time to rectify his misassumption, Cookie waved a tattooed arm toward the back of the house. "Best get on down there. I hear your man call-ing you."

"Your man" instead of "your patient." A funny turn of words. Jett was no more her man than he would ever be any woman's. The fact that they'd spent a fun after-noon at the Pizza Palace meant nothing. Nor did the fact that Dylan talked about the outing constantly and had asked if Jett had any little boys of his own. Just what she didn't need—Dylan to start thinking of Jett as daddy material. The idea was too ridiculous to ponder.

As she ventured down the long hallway, Jett's pleasant baritone filled the air. "'He's got the whole world in his rope…'"

Spirits suddenly lifted, Becka stopped at the closed door to smile at the change of lyrics. What was that nutty cowboy doing in there?

Following a warning knock, she pushed the door open in time to see a coiled lariat sail across the room and encircle the bedpost. Jett reclined in his PT machine, trying to jiggle the rope loose.

At her entrance, he looked up and grinned. "Hey, Becka-Rebecka. What's up?"

Ignoring the zip of energy she experienced every time she walked into a room where he was, Becka went to the bedpost and slid the rope free.

"How long have you been in the machine today?"

He squinted toward the clock. "Five hours and fifty minutes. Ten minutes to go." Jett recoiled the length of hemp before making another single loop, ready to toss again. "You wanna dance? It'll make the time go faster."

"I'll pass." She turned and reached into her bag for her stethoscope. No way she'd let Jett know how much she would enjoy feeling his arms around her again.

"No, you won't."

Before she had time to see what was coming, a rope swished over her head and slid down to her waist, effectively pinning her arms to her sides. She couldn't help it. A surge of excitement stirred her blood and she laughed.

Jett tugged, pulling her backward until she stood beside his recliner looking down into a too-handsome face. Blue eyes glittered with amusement—and something more.

"Dance with me, Becka-Rebecka."

Her heart clattered against her rib cage. "Too risky."

"Okay, then. You asked for it." Giving a quick yank, he unbalanced her, plunging her into his lap. His arms went around her, reinforcing the rope. He snugged her against his chest and grinned down into her face. "Gotcha."

She struggled, but not nearly enough. While the sensible portion of her mind said get up and run, every other cell in her body refused to obey. Jett's cologne—Cool Water, she thought—drifted up from his cotton T-shirt. His firm naked thighs pressed against her trapped fingertips, and she could scarcely keep from stroking the firm, dark flesh.

"When you turn me loose you're going to be very sorry."

"Then I guess I might as well enjoy this while I can." His face moved closer, blue eyes teasing above the dark stubble of five-o'clock shadow. One strong hand slid up the back of her neck to massage the nape. "You've got a knot right there."

"Trust me. I know that. Now let me up."

"Nah. I like having you under my control." He grinned his lascivious grin as his strong hands kneaded the tight neck muscles and snaked beneath her ponytail. "I've been wanting to do this."

Tugging at the scrunchie, he loosened her hair, then used his hard fingers as a comb to smooth the waves over her shoulders. Reaching up, he began a slow, tantalizing massage of her scalp.

Eyes closing in pure pleasure, Becka's head lolled back, her professional reserve disappearing along with the tension in her neck. Touching Jett, being touched by him felt so right.

"Oh my, that feels good."

"Beautiful." The timbre of his voice deepened. "So soft."

His warm breath puffed enticingly against the curve of her neck. She jerked her eyes open to find him close—too close. His blue eyes drifted over her face, coming to rest on her mouth.

Becka's pulse reached mach speed. "Don't even think about it, cowboy."

"Oh, I've been thinking about it a lot lately." His lips inched closer until his next words whispered against her mouth. "And now I'm going to do something about it."

In the next heartbeat he brushed his mouth gently, teasingly across hers then drew back. Disappointment, totally unwelcome, shifted through Becka. The mouth that tantalized lifted at the corners and came back for more.

This time he kissed her—really kissed her—and she wanted her hands free. She wanted to touch him, to pull him closer. To run her fingers through his dark, springy hair and over his strong chest.

The kiss was brief but thorough, and when Jett pulled away, eyes sexy and lazy, his rapid breathing matched her own.

When Becka found her voice, she squeaked, "Don't ever do that again."

Jett quirked an eyebrow; the knowing smile lingered around his tempting lips. "Why? Don't you like me?"

Becka wasn't fool enough to deny the truth. "That's the problem. You're not my type."

"Really? I think maybe you're wrong."

"Let me up." She wiggled, but the movement only succeeded in pressing her bottom deeper into his lap and giving her fingertips a better feel of his thighs.

"I think you want me to kiss you again."

"That will not happen." No matter how much she wanted it.

"What if you change your mind?"

"What if I don't?"

"I do love a challenge."

"Then arm wrestle me."

This time he laughed. "A man has a reputation to maintain. Think what the other guys would say if you beat me."

"Chicken." She hoped the taunt would defuse the romantic tension.

But she couldn't deny how alive and vital that kiss had made her feel, as if a part of her had been in suspended animation since Chris's death. Nor could she deny how much she wanted him to kiss her again.

"Tell you what." Gently holding her by a lock of hair that he stroked over and over again as if it were pure silk, Jett said, "I'll let you go on one condition."

"What's that?"

"You agree to drive my truck until I'm back on my feet."

"We've had this discussion before."

"Not while you were tied up on my lap."

Fighting the pure fun of bantering with joyriding Jett, Becka struggled to regain control. This unbalanced, dancing-on-the-edge-of-the-cliff feeling made her nerves raw. She couldn't let herself enjoy the flight because she couldn't bear the inevitable crash landing.

"Come on Becka-Rebecka. You keep nagging me to stay off my feet. If you don't take my truck, I'm going to drive into town every evening to get you. So, unless you want to be responsible for ruining my knee and my career and stealing my chance to make the NFR, you'd better agree."

The man was as stubborn as the battery in her beat-up old car. She knew he wasn't kidding. He'd be up on that leg, risking his health, and she'd be to blame. Some nurse she was.

His fingers softly stroked the column of her throat. If she didn't get off his lap soon, she was going to make a fool of herself.

"Okay. You win. This time. I'll take your truck, but I have a condition of my own."

Jett groaned. "Why do I have a feeling this means more torture instead of more kissing?"

"Because you're smarter than you look. Fifty leg presses." Becka felt immensely better. She was regaining control of the situation. "Now untie me."

He nuzzled his nose in her hair. "Hmm. Maybe not."

Before she threw caution to the wind and succumbed, Becka tilted to the side, escaping him. "I brought you a present."

He paid her no mind.

"You'll like it," she cajoled in the same way she would convince Dylan to try a new food. "I promise."

With a lusty sigh, he relented. "Spoilsport."

He loosened the lasso and helped her slide the loop over her head. Strong hands encircled her waist as he lifted her off his lap and set her on her feet. "Not another torture device, I hope."

"I brought one of those, too, but we'll get to that later." She gave him a cheeky grin and went to her bag. "This is something to improve your aim."

She pulled out a plastic-covered box and tossed it into his lap. A wide grin broke over his face.

"Sweet. A dart gun."

"Complete with an attached string so all you have to do is yank and the dart pops off the board and returns to you. And your knee is not traumatized in the process."

As soon as she'd seen the toy, she'd thought of Jett and couldn't resist the purchase. All day she'd looked forward to his reaction. He loved games, challenges and anything else that elevated his blood pressure. Becka understood better than most his need for constant activity. She'd once been the same. Sympathy, that's what she felt, though she wanted him to believe she'd brought the toy to keep him off his feet.

Turning the box over in his hands, he looked up at her, expression serious. "Thanks."

"You're welcome." She drew in a lungful of air, relieved to find her equilibrium returning. "Now let's get on with the torture treatments. You want this immobilizer off next week, don't you?" She indicated the metal cage framing his knee.

"I don't know. Being into heavy metal sort of appeals to me."

"Then you'll love my other present. I brought my weight machine today. Cookie said we could set up a minigym in the den for daily workouts."

He perked up. "Are we working out together?"

"As a matter of fact, yes. You're taking up all my time and I'm getting out of shape." She flexed her bicep, perceiving a weakness. "Just look at that."

"I'm looking, I'm looking." The ornery cowboy ignored the muscle, letting his gaze travel slowly over her yellow scrubs instead. Becka's skin grew unreasonably warm. "Did you bring your workout shorts?" he asked. "Please say you did. I'd love to get all sweaty with you."

"For that crack, I'm going to make you do leg curls *and* presses." She sat opposite him, palms out. "Put your foot against my hand. Presses first."

He made a rude noise but did as she asked. Becka laughed then wished she hadn't. She couldn't let him think she was having a good time. That one kiss had nearly unglued her and had almost broken through her force field of hard-won control. This was exactly the reason she hadn't wanted to take this job. She couldn't be trusted in the company of untamed, unpredictable men.

But all the time she worked him, driving him ruthlessly to do more physical therapy than ever before, every fiber in her body was aware of him—of his masculine scent, his hard-cut body, his quirky humor. Even after they moved into the den and began a rigorous regimen of bench presses, crunches and curls, she kept recalling that too-brief kiss, replaying the rush of emotion so many times she blushed. Fortunately the sweat beading her forehead provided the perfect cover.

She kept pace with him, exercise for exercise, working her muscles to exhaustion. But her mind wouldn't shut down.

She kept thinking of Jett's insistence that she drive his truck and wondered why he would offer such a thing. Did he care? Was he trying to protect her and Dylan?

Or was he, as she suspected, generous for his own selfish purposes. He needed her here as his nurse.

"Five more," she puffed. "Work those quads. Remember, the harder we work, the sooner you can return to the rodeo circuit."

"Bring it on, darlin'." He strained, keeping up with her every rep. Sweat beaded his forehead. She knew he hurt, but he'd never say so. "I've never been so ready to leave a place in my life."

Getting on his feet faster was the reason he hired her. So why should reminders of that depress her now?

Becka closed her eyes in frustration. Some perverse part of her wanted him to care.

"Two more," she said, counting down. "One more. Done."

Exhausted but energized, she collapsed onto the floor beside the weight machine. Lying flat on his stomach, Jett peeked over the side. Holding on to his knee, he rolled awkwardly down beside her. He stretched full length on his back, arms thrown out to each side. The right one grazed her hair.

"You're killin' me, woman," he said, breath coming in rapid puffs. "I didn't know I'd gotten so out of shape,"

"It only takes a couple of weeks of inactivity."

"You're not breathing as hard as I am."

"I'm in better shape."

"Ouch. There's goes my ego." He turned his head to look at her. Her insides did a cartwheel. "How long have you been doing this? The fitness training, I mean."

"I first started working out to get in shape after Dylan was born. Then I discovered I had a knack for the training aspect and started working toward certification."

"Was that after your husband died?" His blue eyes were gentle, maybe even concerned. She felt disconcerted by both.

"Yes."

Rattlesnake was a small town. She wasn't surprised that he knew about Chris's death. But she was surprised at how easily she could talk to Jett about it. That day had always been too painful to discuss with anyone.

"He was a fun guy."

"You remember him?"

"Everyone remembers Crazy Chris Washburn. The guy lived life to the fullest."

"Did he?" Tossing an arm over her eyes, she couldn't keep the bitterness from her voice. "I wouldn't call getting killed at age twenty-five living life to the fullest."

Jett rolled toward her. Lying on one side, so close she could feel his body heat, he stroked a finger up and down the sensitive underside of her arm. She knew she should move away, but his comfort and kindness drew her.

"One thing I know for certain, Becka. Life is a risk. You can hide in terror and hope nothing bad ever happens, or you can grab on for the wild, exciting ride. Either way, life is going to happen, both the bad and the good."

Becka knew he was right in part, but she had a son

to consider. Being watchful and diligent and careful was the only way to keep him safe.

"I never dreamed I'd be raising a son alone."

"What did you dream of?" His voice was soft, low, mesmerizing.

Lifting her arm, she met his blue, blue gaze. "That's a funny question."

A tiny smile tipped the corner of his mouth. He seemed determined to touch her, smoothing back the sweat-damp hair from her forehead, his fingers lingering.

"Everybody has dreams, Becka-Rebecka. What are yours?"

Drawing in a deep sigh, she said, "Raising my son to be a good man."

"And you will. But what about you personally? Don't you have dreams for you?"

"Not anymore."

He traced the side of her jaw. "Sad. Everyone needs a star to shoot for."

He was right. A life without dreams had no direction. And that was her. She'd been a rudderless ship for a long time now.

"Most women want a husband, a home, a family. Don't you want any of that?"

Odd that Jett Garrett, confirmed bachelor, lover of all womankind but no one woman, would ask such a thing.

"Sure. Someday. Dylan needs a man in his life. And I'd like more kids. Lots of kids." Her mood lifted at that, thinking of more Dylans to love. But she didn't say the other part. That she wanted to be loved.

Rising on one elbow, she turned toward him. His warm scent of manly perspiration and hard, strong body stirred her senses. A five-o'clock shadow had caught up with him, adding to his sexy, dangerous aura. His dark hair, damp from the workout, was mussed in the most appealing manner. No doubt about it. Jett was glorious to look at and tempting to be around.

"What about you?" She asked. "Besides the NFR, what are your dreams? You can't ride bulls forever."

"One thing at a time, Becka." He tapped her nose. "Once I make the NFR—and I will—I'll formulate a new goal. There will always be mountains to climb, boats to race, horses to ride. Right now, making the NFR is the one that matters."

Staring down into the handsomest face she'd ever seen, Becka suffered an undeniable sense of sadness. Nothing and no one in Jett's life would ever be as important as his need for the next thrill.

Chapter Seven

Jett led the paint gelding out of the barn and into the pleasant September sunshine. He hadn't been on a horse in weeks, and if the docs in Amarillo had their way, he wouldn't get on one for another four weeks. But they had given him permission to begin some light weight bearing, and he figured if he could mount with his good leg, he could ride.

He was getting itchy. Fact of the matter, he'd been itchy since the day he'd messed up and kissed Becka-Rebecka. What started out as teasing had unnerved him. From that day on, her undeniable, irresistible allure nagged at him day and night. Being with her and Dylan felt right—a totally irrational sensation that proved just how messed up he was. No wonder he was itchy.

His leg itched, too, even now that the heavy metal had been replaced by an air splint. But the healing surgical wound wasn't driving him nuts. Becka was.

She flitted in every evening, smelling so sweet and looking so good, he wanted to lasso her again. She'd let down her guard, at least a little, and their conversations had grown deeper, more personal. Now he wasn't sure breaking through her reserve had been his most brilliant idea. The better he knew her, the more he wanted her around.

One kiss and a little conversation had tilted his thinking and he didn't much like the feeling. If the woman would just go to bed with him, the problem would be solved.

Patting the old horse, he longed to throw his leg over the saddle and ride like a Hollywood stuntman. This inactivity was killing him. He was missing too many chances to compete. And he was having too many uncharacteristic thoughts.

When he'd been lying on the floor beside her that day, so close he could count the freckles on her nose, the most aberrant idea had crossed his warped mind. What, he wondered, would it be like to lie beside Becka-Rebecka every night and wake up with her beside him every morning.

The sound of a vehicle crunching up the gravel drive drew his attention, thankfully away from Becka. His sister-in-law pulled her red SUV to a stop and opened the door.

More than eight months' pregnant, Kati took a minute to ease down from the oversize vehicle. Then she released Evan and Dylan from car seats in the back. Both boys made a beeline for Jett.

"Hey, guys." The three males exchanged hand slaps. "You're early."

Kati came up alongside him, looking cool and radiant and unbelievably pregnant. "I had an appointment with my OB this afternoon so we decided to come on home and let Maxine close up the center tonight."

Jett hitched a thumb toward Dylan. The boy stood three feet away, mouth open, staring with undisguised longing at the horse. Jett knew exactly how he felt. "Does Becka know you brought him out here early?"

"I called her. She was okay with it."

"She trusts you."

"She'll trust you, too. Give her some time." Kati smoothed her long fingers down the horse's muzzle. "She's afraid something will happen to Dylan if she isn't careful enough. She was pregnant with him when her husband died, you know."

"Yeah, she told me." He supposed her fear was justified, given the things she'd revealed, but for some weird reason, he wanted to help her get past that. He squinted at Kati. How could his sister-in-law know that he wanted Becka to trust him? He'd only just realized it himself. Avoiding her too-wise eyes, he pretended to adjust the horse's halter. "Hard to believe someone as careful as Becka was married to Crazy Chris Washburn."

"Not really. Becka was once almost as fearless as Chris. The accident changed all that. From what I understand they'd had a few beers and Chris was riding a wave runner with his usual reckless abandon. Becka was with him."

"Anybody who spent much time with Crazy Chris had a reason to be afraid. The guy even scared me. He took enormous risks without considering the consequences." He wondered if Becka realized that.

"And you don't?"

"No. I don't. I always know exactly what I'm doing,

the worst- and best-case scenarios. Chris didn't think before he acted. He'd do anything, anytime for a thrill." He shifted his weight against the side of the horse and glanced at the massive watermelon bulging around her middle. "What did your doc say? Everything okay with the baby?"

"All is well. A few more weeks and you'll be an uncle again." Smiling serenely, she laid a hand on the watermelon. Jett couldn't imagine a tiny human being floating around in there, but he liked thinking about it.

"And Colt will be a daddy." Man, that really blew his mind. His once confirmed-bachelor brother a dad twice over.

"I just hope baby doesn't rush things while Colt is gone to that livestock sale."

"What sale?" Hadn't Colt been to an auction in Amarillo a couple of weeks ago?

"The registered Angus bull sale down in Austin next week. Didn't he mention it to you?"

"No." But then Colt knew his rambling brother paid little attention to ranching business and probably wouldn't care. The funny thing was Jett did care. "Colt has no business running off somewhere with the baby this close."

"Oh, we'll be fine. Don't fret." She waved a dismissing hand and swung her braid over one shoulder. "What did your doctors say today? I see you no longer have a birdcage around your knee."

"Nope. Got me a splint now. And the doc thinks my knee is rehabbing well, thanks to my personal slave driver. I'll be back on the road in a week or two." Right after he had a long talk with his big brother.

She frowned. "Did the doctor tell you that?"

Actually, the doc had said the next few weeks were crucial, but he couldn't wait that long. Fortunately, the two preschoolers saved him from lying to his favorite sister-in-law.

"Mama, I'm hungry." Evan said.

"Maybe Cookie baked muffins." Kati swatted playfully at the dark-haired boy's bottom. "Head into that house, mister, and check it out."

She turned to Dylan who'd sidled up beside Jett and latched on to his hand. "Don't you want to go in for a snack, Dylan?"

"I want to ride the horse with Jett."

She shook her head. "Maybe we should wait and ask your mommy."

Dylan popped a thumb into his mouth but didn't budge from Jett's side.

"Leave him out here, Kati. I'll watch him."

"You sure you don't mind?"

"Mind? He's my bud."

"Don't put him on that horse."

"I hear ya."

Jett waited until the door closed behind Kati and Evan before swinging Dylan into his arms. "You have to know the rules to ride a horse."

Dylan's eyes lit up. The thumb came out of his mouth. "Okay."

For the next few minutes, Jett walked the child through a minilesson in horse safety. "And never, ever go near a horse without an adult," he finished up. "Ready to sit in the saddle?"

Dylan nodded eagerly.

"Hold on to the saddle horn, right here." Jett patted the apparatus. "And I'll hold you from down here. Okay?"

Jett could feel the child's heart pitty-patting beneath his hands as he lifted him into place. Dylan's excitement pleased him. Nothing like that very first horseback ride. He wished he had a camera to capture the moment for Becka.

Then again, maybe not.

The gentle old paint stood patiently as Jett had known he would. Only a torpedo could startle Skipper, and then the horse would simply stop dead still and wait for instructions.

"How do you like it up there, ace?"

"I'm big."

Jett laughed and the child's giggle rang out in response. Over the sound came the thundering rumble of a too-familiar set of mufflers—his own. A glance down the driveway made Jett wince.

Becka.

His pickup truck crunched to a stop and was still rocking when the red-haired tigress flew out the door and stormed across the yard. Dust swirled around her small, white-sneakered feet.

"Get him off there. Get him off!" Her screeching voice trembled with terror.

Dylan started to cry.

Jett wondered how the whole world had gone hysterical in a matter of seconds. For a control freak, Becka displayed an enormous amount of passion when angry.

With a weary sigh, he lifted the boy off the horse and turned to face the consequences.

Dylan ran to his mother, latched on to her pant leg and sobbed.

One hand holding her baby closer, Becka grabbed Jett's arm. The heat of her trembling hand burned into him. "What do you think you're doing?"

"I was only letting the boy sit on a horse. There's no harm in that."

"No harm?" Her voice elevated a notch. "He could have been killed. How could you be so irresponsible?"

Anger, usually a foreign emotion to Jett, pressed at the back of his throat. "I'd never let anything happen to Dylan. Now see to him before he gets as hysterical as you are."

"I am not hysterical. Nor am I finished with you." She bent to the thumb-sucking child whose face was contorted and tearful and took him in her arms. "You're okay now, baby. Mommy's here."

If he had an extra leg to stand on, Jett would have kicked something. The kid had been fine until Becka came screaming at him.

With steely control and awkward movements, given the state of his knee, Jett leaned toward the boy. "Hey, bud. Why don't you go inside and have some muffins with Evan and Cookie so your mom and I can talk?"

Sniffing and trying hard to control his sobs, Dylan's uncertain gaze vacillated between the adults.

Becka burned Jett with a withering stare before saying to Dylan, "Go on, baby. I'll be there in a minute." Under her breath, she muttered, "After I commit a murder."

Still sucking his thumb, Dylan reluctantly left them.

As soon as he disappeared into the house, Becka turned on Jett like a cornered cat. She shoved a finger into his chest and hissed. "You may not care about your own life but you have no right to endanger an innocent child."

Jett didn't much like having a female stab him in the chest. "And you have no business terrorizing him into a sissy. The kid can't even be a normal boy."

Her nostrils flared. "At least he'll be alive."

"You call this living? Crying over everything? Terrified to move because he might get hurt? That's not living, Becka. And it's totally unfair to Dylan."

"Don't try to tell me how to live my life or how to raise my son."

Jett's patience snapped. "Somebody needs to because you don't live at all. You exist. You're afraid to live, afraid to feel."

"What would you know about feeling? You've never watched someone you love take his last breath because he thought the only way to live was on the edge."

"At least he knew how it felt to be really alive. You run from your house to your job, waiting for the sky to fall, hovering over Dylan until he can't even breathe. Do you know he never sucks his thumb unless you're around? *You* make him afraid, insecure. He was laughing when I put him on that horse and you scared him to death with your screaming."

"How dare you! How dare you judge me? I love my son. He's my whole life, my reason for being. I go out of my mind worrying that he's inherited the same deadly behavior patterns that killed his father." Tears glistened in her eyes. "And then you come along, as out-of-control and irresponsible as Chris and encourage Dylan to take dangerous risks."

That hurt. And he was tired of being called irresponsible. He liked his fun and he liked to push the envelope, but he had never endangered anyone but himself.

"I'm sorry about your husband, Becka, but you know what? I'm not him. Chris did insane things without ever considering the risks for himself or anyone else. I'm not like that. I would never intentionally put Dylan or you in any real danger. Never."

"Are you saying Chris didn't care about me?" She looked stricken, distraught. And he hated that.

A lump the size of a buffalo pushed against his lungs. It took him a second or two to find his voice and when he did, he couldn't stop the words that formed. "A man would be a fool not to care about you."

Becka stilled, staring at him with the oddest expression in her honey-brown eyes. "What do you mean by that?"

He didn't know, and he sure as heck didn't want to think about it.

"Look, Becka, it was only a horseback ride. I didn't mean to upset you. Truce, okay?" He touched her arm in apology. "I shouldn't have put Dylan on the horse without your permission."

Becka relented. At his quiet words and simple apology, all the fury drained away and took the fear along with it. "My father thinks I'm making a sissy out of him, too."

"He's your son. How you raise him is your business."

Could the way she was raising him be the cause of his fears, of his nightmares, his thumb sucking? She wanted to protect her child, not make him afraid. "He looks up to you, admires you."

That fact troubled her some. Why couldn't Dylan admire someone less...vital?

"He's a great kid."

"But you think he's a wuss?" The use of his term for a sissy brought a smile.

"Boys need to play rough and rowdy, Becka. We're programmed by nature to run and jump and compete. That's why we play sports. Being all boy doesn't necessarily mean he'll turn out like Chris."

"You think I'm overprotective."

The corners of his mouth tipped. "Loosening up a little wouldn't hurt anything."

She knew he was right. "I'm sorry I screamed at you. I get so scared…"

"Let him ride the horse, Becka."

Her pulse skittered at the thought of her baby on that massive animal. "Is this the horse Evan rides?"

"All by himself. Old Skipper is the gentlest horse I've ever known."

"Will you hold him the entire time?" She couldn't believe she was actually considering this.

"Every second. Trust me, Becka."

Trust him? Trust a man who'd once made his own bungee cord and plunged off the town water tower?

"What do ya say? Dylan's been begging to ride for days."

Becka knew that was true. The child rattled constantly about the horses and cows and tractors. His attraction to the ranch—and Jett—was obvious.

A horsefly buzzed in, landing on the horse's neck. Jett's resulting slap echoed loudly, but Skipper never flinched.

Becka sucked in a huge breath. Maybe the argument had rattled her thinking. Maybe she should get in her own car and never come back. But she knew she wouldn't. Because, right this minute, her son was going to experience his very first horseback ride. And she was going to watch, even if it terrified her.

Much later, after Dylan's short, ecstatic ride; after a vigorous workout that left Becka as weary and relaxed as Jett; and after a pleasant meal at Cookie's table, Becka sat on the patio with the three Garrett adults, sipping iced tea and watching the sunset. Dylan and Evan played trucks in the sandbox.

A dozen thoughts flickered in and out of her mind. The fight with Jett had been almost…invigorating. How long had it been since she'd allowed herself to let go that way? She supposed that was a bad sign, an indication that Jett brought out the worst in her. But watching Dylan take his first horseback ride had been worth the trouble.

Even though she'd fought down a roaring case of nerves, she was glad she'd given in. Jett had shown exquisite care, gently teaching and encouraging the boy as if he was his own. And most of all he'd protected him, holding a hand on the reins and on Dylan every single minute of the ride.

Inside the kitchen behind them came the rattle of dishes. Becka started up from the lawn chair. "Maybe I should go in and offer Cookie some help with the cleanup."

Jett caught her arm. "Forget it. Nobody messes around in Cookie's kitchen."

"Except Kati," Colt said, sliding an arm around his very pregnant wife.

Kati, the picture of maternal serenity, smiled. "He doesn't even allow me in there lately."

"That's because you're pregnant," Jett said. "Cookie pampers you more than Colt does."

"Hey," Colt said, pretending insult. "I do my share of pampering. Don't I, sweetheart?"

Becka watched the exchange of glances between the married couple and envied them the special intimacy their look revealed. Here were two people who'd found their perfect mates.

Curled on the air-conditioning unit, a sleek gray cat blinked interested yellow eyes at a pair of humming-birds darting around Cookie's feeders. Out in the sand-box, the two boys made competing motor sounds while the adults chatted and the sun, trailing red and orange, slipped below the horizon.

Soon Colt rose. "Sorry to break up the party, but I have a little office work to do before bedtime."

His wife rose beside him. "And I'm worn out tonight for some reason."

Everyone smiled at the remark. Kati's advanced state of pregnancy coupled with the work she did at the day care was enough to exhaust three women.

Holding hands, Kati and Colt said good-night and sauntered into the house, leaving Jett and Becka with the boys. The cat leaped down from his perch and followed.

In the dusky sky the first stars appeared. And in the distance, barely outside the glow of the house lights, a few lightning bugs flickered, eager to find a mate.

Jett braced his arms behind his head and stretched. "Even the air smells good tonight."

Becka sipped at the cool, sweet tea to avoid looking

at Jett's pose. During their workouts, she managed an objective distance, ignoring the pulse of attraction that simmered constantly between them. But these moments outside of therapy made her so aware of him. "Fall is in the air. I love this time of year."

The evening breeze felt good against her skin, promising cooler temperatures later on. She was glad for the sweats and T-shirt she'd changed into.

"Me, too. Usually." Jett's hands fell to his lap. His jaunty attitude fell with them. He stared solemnly out at the children.

Becka guessed his dilemma. "This is a big time of year for rodeo, isn't it?"

"Yeah. The NFR is a couple of months away. If I don't get back on the circuit soon, my chances are toast."

"Can't you let the knee heal completely and try again next year?"

He shook his head. "I've never been this close before. This is the year. If I don't do it now, I never will."

His mood surprised and concerned her. "Where's that optimism of yours tonight?"

"Oh, I'm still optimistic, or I wouldn't be planning to ride again this season. But I know my body. Each year the injuries have gotten worse and taken longer to heal. Age is tough on an athlete."

"What will you do if this is the end? If you can't go back?"

He cut her a sharp look. "Don't even think that. The docs say we're doing a great job rehabbing. If everything goes perfectly for the next few weeks, the knee will be recovered enough for me to get back on the road. I have to go. I need to go."

She couldn't bear to think of him hurt again—or worse yet, killed like Chris. And maybe that was the problem plaguing her lately. She didn't want him to leave because she feared for him. "Why does the NFR matter so much? You don't need the work or the money."

"I don't know. Maybe to prove that I can. To do something that most men can't."

"Some people would say you live dangerously for the attention."

"Probably." Turning toward her with a soft chuckle, he smoothly moved the subject away from his reasons for living a daredevil life. A man like Jett didn't want to look too deep. "How's the truck holding up? Any problems?"

"It's heaven on four wheels." Becka toasted him with her tea glass. "The AC works all the time. The battery is never dead. And the engine has never overheated." She laughed softly. "I didn't know such a vehicle existed."

She didn't want to mention that every time she climbed inside the cab his presence overwhelmed her. The scent of his cologne. His oddball collection of music—cowboy barroom tunes and southern gospel with a dollop of heavy metal thrown into the confusion. Music as complex as the man. Everything about the truck screamed of him and made her think of him far more than was wise.

"I can't thank you enough for letting me drive it."

He patted the splint encasing his shorts-clad leg. "You already have. I'm too lazy to work this hard unless somebody forces me to."

Becka shook her head, knowing him well enough now to realize that was not true. Jett Garrett might be restless, but he wasn't lazy.

Darkness had descended and the two youngsters tumbled out of the sandbox and headed toward the house.

"Where are you boys going?" Becka called.

"I gotta potty." Evan grabbed the front of his shorts. Dylan did likewise. "Me, too."

"Go on, then. And don't forget to wash your hands."

Holding her tea glass, she rose, following the boys as far as the awning post. The sudden absence of their happy chatter left the outdoors too quiet.

Jett broke the silence. "Thanks for letting him ride the horse today. For trusting me to take care of him."

For trusting him? Had she? Becka blinked down at him, shocked to realize that for the few minutes while her son giggled and glowed from atop Skipper, she had known Jett wouldn't let him fall.

"He loved it." Sipping at the tea, she let the icy drink slide down her throat. When had she begun feeling safe with Jett Garrett?

"Me, too," Jett said. "I liked seeing him excited." He rose too, carefully giving the knee a moment to adjust before moving to the edge of the long, natural-rock patio. "He's a sweet kid, Becka. Chris would be proud of him."

"Chris would call him a sissy, too."

"He'd be wrong. I was wrong. Dylan's a little hesitant maybe, but he's got guts."

"More than I want him to have. Yesterday he ran off from me at Wal-Mart because he wanted to ride the twenty-five-cent horsie and I didn't have time." He'd frightened her senseless running out the door right next to the busy parking lot. But no matter how she'd called, he'd kept running, heading straight for that plastic pony.

"Sometimes I see so much of Chris in him that it scares me to death. What if something happens to him? I can't bear the thought that I could lose him, too."

"Being with Chris the day of the accident must have been hard."

"It was horrible." She shrugged, struggling not to let melancholy thoughts take hold. "I wish we'd never gone to the lake that day. I wish…"

"I remember when it happened. I was in Colorado Springs at the time, but bad news travels in a hurry. Nobody could believe that Crazy Chris was gone."

"He shouldn't have been. If I had been more careful…"

Jett tilted his head to one side, frowning. "You?"

She nodded. "Me. I'm the person responsible for Chris's death."

Instead of denying the truth, as most people would, Jett moved closer to her, trailed one finger down the side of her cheek and said, "What happened?"

An aura of sympathy as warm as the subtle scent of his masculine body emanated from that gentle touch. She and Jett had discussed Chris, had even talked some about his death, but she'd never told a soul the entire story of that day, keeping it locked inside to torment her.

Without understanding why, Becka felt compelled to tell Jett the awful secret she'd never shared with anyone. Under cover of darkness, the words would be easier to say.

"I was careless and stupid… And I killed him."

The words whispered on the night breeze, echoing like the coyote call in a distant pasture. Jett was silent for a long time and she felt his laser eyes peering at her in the faint light from the kitchen behind them.

"Chris's death was an accident, Becka," he said at last.

"No, not an accident." She shook her head when he would have argued. "It wasn't. We did what we did on purpose, foolishly calling it a celebration." She rubbed her hand over the moist tea glass, wishing she could rub away the heavy, aching load of guilt as easily. "We had just confirmed that I was six weeks' pregnant with Dylan. Celebrating a life with a death." A bitter sound escaped her throat. "Chris had even chugged a few beers as a toast."

"What about you?"

"No. No beer." Thank God, she didn't have that added to her load of guilt. "In my warped way, I didn't want to harm my baby. Chris and I played on the lake all the time—wave running, skiing, speed boating. Water sports were our favorite." She missed the water still, though she'd not allowed herself the luxury since Dylan's birth. "We spent nearly every weekend of the summer on the lake, so I never considered the water as a danger to any of us. We were two excellent athletes. Nothing could happen. Or so I thought."

She looked up at Jett, a man who understood danger, and saw his compassion. A lump formed in her throat when he stepped closer, almost as though he could shield her from hurt with his presence.

Comforted, she went on. "Each of us rode our own wave runner. We played chicken all the time, riding toward each other until one of us gave up and turned aside. No one ever got hurt."

She could still picture Chris in that last moment of vivid life—the picture that haunted her dreams. Sandy hair blowing back from his face, the wild laugh that set her blood on fire, the challenge in his eyes as he roared over the water toward her, so alive.

"I don't know what went wrong that day. I was always the one to give in—always. Backing down was not in Chris's vocabulary."

"I remember that much about him. He had an iron will. Nobody could make Chris say uncle."

"He often teased me about chickening out. Told me to toughen up." Suddenly chilled on the inside, she set the glass in the lawn chair cup holder and hugged herself. "I don't know. I've replayed those moments a million times. Somehow I waited too long. By the time I jerked the wheel to miss him, it was too late."

They'd both gone airborne, separated from their respective watercraft like two human cannonballs. "Other than having the breath knocked out of me from hitting the water so hard, I was okay."

"But Chris wasn't."

"No. Chris was—" The old choking guilt threatened her air passages. She swallowed hard. "In reality already dead. Oh, he was on a ventilator for several weeks while we hoped and prayed he'd come out of the coma. But the Chris I knew was gone long before his heart stopped beating."

Jett's fingers stroked her upper arm, softly, gently. He didn't say anything, for which she was grateful, but his touch spoke volumes of understanding and support.

Buoyed, if such a thing was possible, she kept going, eager now to purge the ugliness from her soul. "One of the wave runners hit him in the head. Authorities never figured out which one."

"But you blame yourself." Gently he squeezed the flesh of her biceps.

"Of course I do. I knew Chris. Turning first, backing off was my part of the game. I killed him, Jett. Because I wasn't careful enough. Dylan doesn't have a daddy because of me."

"Chris should never have taken you out there. If my woman was pregnant…" He stopped, slid his hand away from her and rubbed it over his face.

"I need to go home," she said. "Six o'clock arrives early." But she didn't move. She stood there, hugging her own body, wondering what Jett must think of a woman foolhardy enough to jeopardize not only her life but that of her unborn child. A woman who caused the death of her husband in the name of fun.

The dim light from the kitchen played over him, all shadows and blue eyes. Jett was a man she could find in the deepest darkness. A personality that cast his own white-hot light. A man whose energy generated enough power to light a small city.

A man so like Chris—and yet so different. She knew that now, in a way she hadn't before. Chris would have laughed at her guilt. Jett had been a solid shoulder, absorbing her pain as if he could make her suffering go away. A fragment of her sorrow winged off into the night.

"Pushing the envelope is a part of some people, Becka," he said at last. "Of Chris. And me. Of you, too. Chris made his own choices. And you didn't do anything except behave like the exciting, spirited woman you are."

She shook her head in denial. "I don't want to be like that anymore. It's too risky."

"But you are like that," he said softly, tugging at her hands, pulling her toward him. His voice fell to a whisper on the night wind. "Hiding your light doesn't keep it from shining."

A shiver danced over her. His warm hands rubbed her arms, sliding up until he enfolded her. She went willingly, needing his comfort, or so she told herself.

"I'm sorry about Chris. I'm sorry for all the heartache you've been through." Cradling her against his shoulder, he stroked her hair, then made small, soothing circles on her backbone.

Becka wrapped her arms around his waist and rested her head on his chest, feeling more secure than she had in a long time. Security and Jett didn't belong in the same sentence, and yet she could think of no other way to describe her emotions.

"Men like Chris and me make our own choices, Becka. No matter how hard you've worked at rehabbing my knee, if I decide tomorrow to get on a bull, there won't be a thing you can do to stop me. Chris was the same way."

She shook her head. "I know. But getting past the guilt is still hard." The smooth cotton of Jett's T-shirt caressed her cheek. Beneath her ear, his lion's heart beat, strong and sure.

"But you can. For Dylan's sake, as well as your own. You have to learn to let go, to be who you really are. And to let Dylan be who he really is." Becka suspected he was right, but fear was a hard taskmaster.

He pulled back slightly, gazing down into her upturned face. She could see the wheels turning in his head and realized she'd let things go too far. He was too near, the conversation too personal, and he was too much man for her.

Every moment spent this close to Jett brought her closer to believing he cared for her. And that was a fool's game.

"I really do need to go."

"No. Not yet." Strong, athletic hands caressed her face.

Every muscle in her body began to quiver in response to his touch, his nearness, his vitality.

The questions that sizzled between them constantly refused to be sublimated any longer.

"You're doing funny things to my head, Becka. I want you," he murmured right before he proved his words with a kiss.

He'd kissed her before, that teasing promise, but this was promise fulfilled.

His heart slammed against her, jump-starting her own.

Becka's control snapped like an electric line in a tornado. She'd been on the verge of losing control since the moment she'd spotted Dylan perched high on that horse. But she could deal with losing control of anger. This had nothing to do with anger, or even with the ugly guilt she'd poured at Jett's accepting feet.

This was passion, pure and engulfing—the very emotion she'd sworn was no longer in control. But she could no more stop her eager response to Jett's mouth than she could bench-press a Brahma bull.

He had delicious lips. Firm and warm and full of suggestion. Oh, and she longed to follow those suggestions. How many times since he'd first kissed her had she wanted it to happen again? She wanted to lose herself in him, to forget all the hurt and guilt and fear, and go with the pleasure.

Once she'd watched a man swimming against the

current, but though he'd battled and struggled, the water had sucked him under. She felt that way now, but there was no lifeguard to rescue her from herself. And right this lovely moment, she didn't want to be rescued. She wanted to feel.

When the kiss ended, Jett looked as thunderstruck as she felt. Her knees shook and a hot flash burned her body. Shocked at her behavior, Becka touched her fingertips to lips still moist and achy.

For years she'd carefully sublimated her passionate nature, the dangerous side of her personality—the part of her that could get a man killed. But one hungry kiss from a man like Jett and she was out of control. Why? Had his compassion, his willingness to listen and console destroyed her common sense?

She jerked away. "I told you not to do that anymore."

A pleased-with-himself tilt of those delicious lips. "Must be the concussion acting up. I forgot."

"Don't forget again." Breathless, almost panting, she stared wildly about, wishing for an escape. But she couldn't escape herself.

A crease appeared between his eyes.

"Don't go." He moved as if to take her in his arms again. Becka backed away. If he touched her, she wasn't at all sure she could resist.

"Come on, Becka-Rebecka," he cajoled, his voice low and husky. "We're both unattached. We can play if we want to."

Was that what he wanted? To play with her as if she were a toy to use and then discard? The words were like a knife in her gut. She didn't want to play around with Jett, then have him leave her alone and empty. She wanted…

Oh, no.

Her pulse rate took another jolt of adrenaline. She grabbed the patio post and wished for the strength to rip it out of the ground and hit herself over the head. She could not, would not fall in love with Jett. No, no, no. But the danger signs were all around, and if she didn't get away from him soon, she would get her heart broken.

Seizing upon the first thing that came in her head, Becka said, "But I'm not unattached. I'm…seeing someone."

Jett's eyes narrowed, spearing her as though he could see the lie. "You can't mean that Benton guy I met at your house."

"Benchley. And yes. He wouldn't like the idea of another man kissing me, now that we're seeing so much of each other." It was only a small lie. She had seen Sherman a couple of times this week for about fifteen minutes total. But seeing more of him suddenly sounded like a good idea. No matter how her heart protested, she needed a man who made her feel calm instead of manic. A man who didn't scare her half to death.

"When?" Jett frowned. "You work all day and you're out here nearly every evening. The only time you have left is night…"

He gave her a funny look that said he suspected she was sleeping with Sherman. Becka didn't know whether to laugh or scream. She wasn't sleeping with Sherm. She had a son to consider, but her romantic life was none of Jett's business. However, letting him think such a thing might be the perfect way to make him back off.

"Let's get something straight, Jett. Ours…as in me and you—" she waved a trembling finger back and forth between them "—is a professional relationship. Nothing more. Nothing less. Things have been a little…lax lately." The understatement of the year. "But that must end here and now. I won't be here tomorrow. I have a date."

Even if Sherman was busy tomorrow night, she'd make a date with her dad or her best friend, Shannon. She would have a date tomorrow and it would not be with Jett Garrett. From this moment on, she was reestablishing her professional footing. No more dart games. No more weight room challenges. No more mind-blowing kisses. No more abject fear that she was falling in love with the Texas wild man.

Absolutely none.

Chapter Eight

"You can't do this to me."

Jett was in a near state of panic. He squeezed the telephone receiver until the thing should have snapped in two.

One hot, sizzling, mind-bending kiss and the whole world had fallen off its axis. If he'd known Becka would get so worked up he wouldn't have kissed her that way.

On second thought, he probably would have. He'd known she was full of fire, and feeling the flame rise between them had been worth the hassle she was giving him now. Sort of.

"You know the exercise routine by heart, Jett," her sexy voice purred against his ear. Since when had her voice sounded so tantalizing? "There's no reason for me to come out there every day for four or five hours. Cutting back to one hour every other day makes perfect sense."

"I can't do this alone. I'll fall apart. My knee will lock up. I'll be a cripple."

"You'll go right on working out like always."

How could she sound so calm?

"But you won't be here to make me. You're my slave driver. I'm lazy. I'll give up."

If she was here right now, he'd grab her and kiss some sense into her. He'd make her admit she wanted him as much as he wanted her.

"You will not quit. You are too close to full recuperation and another idiotic bull ride."

She was right, dang it. But he wanted her here. He was certain with a little more time, she'd stop fighting him and they could have some real fun before he had to leave. Besides, the place was too lonely without her snap and sass.

"Why are you doing this? Because I kissed you? Because you kissed me back? Because I made you admit you're a passionate woman?" His questions met with a silence that he took as agreement. "Come on, Becka, it was only a kiss." A kiss that had knocked his hat in the dirt.

She expelled a heavy sigh he could only interpret as annoyance. "I have a life, Jett."

"Oh." That stiff-necked Bentley dude again. He'd hoped she was making that up last night. Apparently not. "Work is cutting in on your love life. Excuse me. I'd forgotten."

"Maybe we should have that concussion checked again. You're forgetting a lot of things lately."

He hadn't sulked since he was ten years old and his mother refused to buy him a Harley. But he felt one coming on now. What was happening to him? Since when had any woman given him so much trouble? And since when had he cared one way or the other? There were plenty of buckle bunnies out there, just waiting for the old Jett to return.

But he didn't want any of them. He wanted an undersize, redheaded tigress who pushed him and harassed him and made him laugh.

Last night he'd experienced something else, too, something unfamiliar, and now his universe was out of line. When Becka had confided in him about Chris's death, he'd wanted to make the world right for her, to fix things so she wouldn't feel so bad anymore.

Man. Had a measly little knee injury taken him all the way over the hill?

He'd felt sorry for her. That's why he'd held her…and kissed her until his eyes crossed. Hey, he was a compassionate guy!

"Jett?" That honeyed voice roused him from his stupor. "I'll return your truck tomorrow, okay?"

A pain twisted in his belly. The stubborn redhead was giving him an ulcer.

He had to get off this phone before he started begging and whining like a hungry coon dog. "Keep the truck."

Before she could argue further, he slammed the phone down. Hobbling up from the kitchen table, he discovered, much to his annoyance, that Cookie had come into the room.

"I thought you were doing laundry."

"Time to cook supper." To prove the point, Cookie turned his back and yanked a mixing bowl from an overhead cabinet.

Jett started toward the door. Kati's gray cat stared up at him from the windowsill as if the creature knew he was miserable. "Don't set places for Becka and Dylan. They aren't coming."

"I heard."

Jett stopped in the doorway and turned around. "That's it? No wisecracks? No sage advice?"

"Not for you." Cookie knocked an egg against the side of the bowl. "Now if Becka was to ask me, I'd tell her to run far and fast."

"You won't have to. She already is." She'd been running from the moment he'd met her.

"Good. A woman like that don't need a playmate to kiss her in the dark, then ride off to a rodeo. She needs a real man." He whipped around and aimed an oversize wooden spoon in Jett's direction. "Something you wouldn't know nothing about."

Jett gave the old cook a sharp glance. Had he seen them kissing last night or was he generalizing?

"Apparently she has a man, Cookie. Which is fine with me. I don't have time to play right now and I'm sure as heck not interested in anything else." He didn't need or want a woman messing with his mind. The fact that she already had was all the more reason to get the heck out of Dodge. "There's a rodeo in Santa Fe in two weeks…and I aim to be there."

Stifling a yawn, Becka tried to concentrate on the movie playing across her small television set. On the couch beside her, dressed in perfectly creased slacks and a golf shirt, sat her date for the evening, Sherman Benchley. Dylan had long since escaped to his room to play. Becka wished she had gone with him.

A date with Sherman never thrilled, but that had been

the point. He was safe and comfortable. However, tonight she was antsy and the fault lay firmly with Jett Garrett. If he hadn't kissed her like that, reminding her of the woman she'd once been, everything would be fine.

But Jett couldn't leave well enough alone. He'd pushed from the start, trying to lure her into his fire, and last night she'd rushed right into the flames, savoring the glorious jolt of electricity running between them. Now today, she could think of little else.

But the sexual attraction wasn't the only thing getting to her. Jett, for all his mischief and showing off, was deeper than he let on. When he'd held and comforted her, some of the old guilt about Chris's accident eased away. Jett's compassion was every bit as alluring as his magnetic personality and incredible body.

Sighing, she stuffed another Chee-to in her mouth and crunched.

Sherman shot her an affronted glance. She had interrupted his running commentary of the film—a commentary that was starting to annoy. He always did this, revealed the surprises before they happened, and the habit was wearing thin.

"Now watch right here, Rebecka." Sherman aimed the remote at the screen. "The gunman is hiding behind the bedroom door."

She wished a gunman was hiding behind her bedroom door. Maybe he'd shoot her and put her out of her misery. Unwanted and unavoidable visions of Jett plagued her mind while Sherman just plain plagued her. In all the time she'd known him, she'd never realized how self-absorbed her insurance man could be. But then, she'd never had Jett as a comparison.

With barely concealed annoyance, Becka said, "You know, Sherman, my eyesight is excellent. I can watch this movie for myself."

Pushing *Pause,* he laid aside the remote to turn in her direction. "Really, Rebecka. You're on the snippy side tonight. That time of the month?"

No question vexed her as much as that one. Gritting her teeth, she replied, "Women get tired and cranky for no specific reasons, Sherman. The same as men."

"You're overtired. I should have known." He grasped her hand in a sympathetic squeeze, his skin as soft as her own—a reminder of Jett's rough but tender touch. "Driving out to that ranch night after night, dealing with that…cowboy." He said the word with distaste. "I know you need the extra cash, but I wish you'd stop."

"I have, essentially. We've cut the therapy sessions back to every other day." A fact that depressed her. She missed Jett's silly singing and his spontaneous playfulness. Glancing up at the tall, stiff man beside her, she wondered if Sherman had ever done a spontaneous thing in his life.

"That's a relief. From his caveman attitude the day I met him, plus the way you were out there so often, I'd begun to think the two of you had something going on."

"Between Jett Garrett and me?" She tried to laugh but settled for a weak *humph* instead. "The man makes me a nervous wreck." That much at least was true and the very reason she was here with Sherman—right where she belonged—with a man whose idea of excitement was underwriting a new life insurance policy. Never mind that she wanted to yank her hand out of his doughy one and tell him to go home.

"You're too trusting for your own good, Rebecka. I saw the territorial gleam in Garrett's eyes when he looked at you, like a wolf guarding his lair. Such men can't be trusted."

An unbidden rush of pleasure winged through her chest. Had Jett really looked at her like that?

She tamped back the response. Sherman was the man for her. Not that their relationship had progressed to such an extent. But he was dependable, steady and predictable. Just the kind of man she required. Life with Sherm would always be under tight control. She and Dylan had nothing to fear. For reasons she didn't want to explore, the idea didn't comfort as it once had.

Dylan, as if beckoned by her thoughts, charged in from the hallway, riding a stick horse.

"Yee-ha," he called, flogging the play horse with one hand as he galloped noisily around the living room.

"Dylan, settle down."

Slowing his pony to a trot, Dylan pulled alongside his mother. "I'm a cowboy like Jett. We ride and rope."

Becka felt Sherman's eyes boring into her from the side.

"That's all fine and dandy, but horseback riding belongs outside."

"That's right, young man," Sherman interjected. "Now if you'll play quietly in your room, I'll see that your mother lets you ride the pony at Wal-Mart tomorrow."

Dylan shook his head. "I ride real horses now. Jett lets me."

Sherman turned toward Becka; his gray eyes appraised her coolly. "Really?"

"Uh-huh." Dylan reached for the Chee-tos, stuffing

too many in his mouth at once. "Someday Jett will get me a horse of my own. When I'm bigger."

"Dylan," Becka admonished, secretly glad her son had provided a diversion from Sherman's prying. She'd had no idea her son thought Jett would provide him with a horse. "One Chee-to at a time."

Grinning a yellow-orange, crumbly smile, Dylan mumbled through the chips, "Okay. Only one." Then, eyes alight with mischief, he shoved another Chee-to into the already bulging mouth.

Becka laughed. "You little scamp."

Sherman didn't find the act amusing. "Really, Rebecka, don't allow him to behave so rudely. Discipline at an early age is essential to proper character development."

She'd heard Sherman's theories on child rearing before. In fact, for Dylan's safety, she'd always agreed with his assessments. But she had a burr under her saddle tonight for some reason and rushed to Dylan's defense.

"Little boys are naturally rowdy and noisy and messy." She couldn't believe she was echoing Jett's sentiments. "And I want Dylan to be a normal child, Sherman, not some mouse with no personality."

Sherman rose from the couch, brushing at his slacks as though her furniture was dusty. "You're not yourself tonight. I think I should leave."

He was right. She wasn't herself, thanks to Jett. That troublesome cowboy had her so mixed up she had hurt the feelings of a nice man.

She followed him to the door. "I'm sorry, Sherman. Truly."

Turning, he favored her with an indulgent expression. "Rest. You're overtaxed. I'll pick you up tomorrow evening around five-thirty, and we'll have a nice quiet dinner at the Roundup."

The mention of dinner at the best restaurant in Rattlesnake brought to mind the fun she and Jett and Dylan had enjoyed at the Pizza Palace. She doubted poor Sherman would prove as entertaining.

"Make that six-thirty and you have a date."

His expression tightened. "Why so late?"

Becka didn't consider a six-thirty dinner particularly late but kept that to herself. She'd said quite enough for one evening. "I have a home health visit after work tomorrow."

"With that cowboy." It was a statement, rendered with a hint of annoyance.

"Yes. But only for an hour. Jett will soon be back on the rodeo circuit and out of my hair forever." The truth formed a tight knot in her chest.

"Not a day too soon."

Without fanfare, Sherman bent to kiss her good-night. His lips were dry and smooth and gentle. And there was nothing wrong with his technique, except that his touch did not move her in the least. No eager trembling. No hunger for more. No burst of flame way down in her belly.

"Good night, Sherm," she said, and watched him cross the small front yard and get into his car. She stood in the doorway for a long time, fingertips against her lips, remembering another kiss. And she wondered, not for the first time tonight, if Jett had ruined her chances for happiness with Sherman.

Jett laid aside the ledger he'd been going over for Colt and stretched his arms overhead. Working the books, exercising like a fiend and prowling around the barn were the only things keeping him sane since Becka's virtual abandonment.

Pushing up from his brother's desk, he headed toward the den. When he'd heard Becka come in, he'd thought making her wait might be fun, but after three minutes he'd sauntered down the hall and into the makeshift fitness center he'd come to think of as "theirs." Trouble was she wouldn't work out with him anymore.

"You look beat," he offered, mustering his cockiest attitude. "Another hot date last night?"

Actually, she looked good—real good. A disturbing notion flickered through his head that old Sherm must do something for the redhead that he didn't. Stupid thought.

Becka placed her blue nurse's bag in the usual spot before appraising him with eyes as brown and cool as a root beer float. He hated that distance she'd put between them. "This tired look is because of you, Jett. I'm weary of your questions. And though it's none of your business, yes, Sherman took me out."

For an entire week, since she'd announced her intention to be his "nurse, not your playmate," she'd buzzed in like a hyperactive mosquito, checked his physical health, ordered him to exercise more, and had flown out of here as if she couldn't wait to escape, leaving him more restless than ever.

"Where did Mr. Entertainment take you?" There was something suspect about a man who never took a woman anywhere worth talking about. What kind of jerk was this Bentley anyway?

Becka bent to check his knee, pressing her fingers

into the soft meat at the sides. Somehow she homed in on the sorest spot, but he refused to complain. Her touch was clinical, impersonal and he didn't like the feeling. He wanted the real Becka.

"Sherman and I went gaming."

"Yeah? Sounds exciting. What kind of games?" He knew some great games of his own if she'd dump Boring Bentley and be the Becka he'd come to know and l…ike.

A faint blush crept over her cheekbones. She pushed a little harder on the knee and murmured, "Bingo," just as he gave up and hissed from the pain.

"I heard that," he grunted, his spirits elevating along with his pain level. "Bingo. As in the Thursday-night bingo game at the Senior Citizens' Hall?"

Old Bentley was a real swinger.

Her chin shot up in a failed attempt at haughtiness. "Sherman's mother enjoys the outing."

"Bingo with the silver set." Jett stifled a fake yawn. "That'll get your blood pumping."

"It was nice."

"Don't you mean boring to the point of coma?"

"There is nothing wrong with a quiet evening in the company of good people."

Satisfaction filled him. Why couldn't she admit that Bentley had the imagination of a hairball and was not the most exciting guy in Texas? He, on the other hand, could provide enough thrills and chills to raise goose bumps on a slab of marble. When would she recognize the truth and dump that guy?

Then again, the idea of a quiet evening, just him and Becka, a little music, a few stars, a lot of romance, sounded pretty good right now.

He frowned. As a matter of fact, the notion sounded way better than anything else he could think of.

An unpleasant thought intruded like a gnat up the nose. Was that the way Becka felt about Bentley? Did simply being with the man make her feel content and energized at the same time?

He scraped a hand over his sandpaper jaws and questioned his sanity. Not once in his life had he ever felt content with a woman for more than a couple of days. But for those few weeks when Becka had been his daily companion, he had been.

This was bad. This was very bad. He was sicker than he thought. Leftovers from the concussion must be causing these aberrations. He was not a one-woman man. Not now. Not ever.

While Jett ruminated, Becka was still stuck in the conversation. "A bingo game can be pretty exciting."

Jett shook off the weird sensation crawling up his backbone and fought for an amused expression.

"Would I doubt you?"

She relented and grinned. "Yes, you would."

"So," he said as casually as he could with this creepy knot in his gut. "Are you and boring Bentley an item now?"

She raised an eyebrow. "That's an interesting term."

"Don't avoid the question." He was surprised at the vehemence in the command, but he had a right to know. Not on a personal level, but she was his nurse. He'd grown fond of her in a brotherly sort of way. And Bentley wasn't good enough for her. She deserved better. Any dude that stiff wouldn't make a good dad for Dylan, either. The idea of old Sherm teaching Dylan to ride or fish or play ball was downright laughable.

"Well?" he demanded.

"I suppose."

A stab of an unfamiliar emotion twisted in his gut. Not jealousy, because he didn't know what that was, but something unpleasant. He figured he'd better change the conversation before he drove into Rattlesnake and damaged his reputation and Sherman Bentley's face all in one quick punch.

Mind working frantically, he said the first thing he could think of. "The doc said I could drive my pickup after this week."

He hadn't meant to tell her that yet. She needed his truck.

She looked up, caught off guard. "When did you talk to Dr. Jameson?"

"Colt had business in Amarillo this morning so I rode along, popped in and paid the doc a surprise visit. He was thrilled to see me."

"Did he say anything about increasing the weight-bearing work?"

"Yep. Got a paper over there somewhere he said to give you." He waved his arm toward the desk. "He thinks the knee is almost healed. If nothing goes wrong, I can make that rodeo in Santa Fe weekend after next."

He didn't bother to admit that Dr. Jameson thought he should lay off at least another three months to be on the safe side. Nor did he tell her of the dire predictions the surgeon had made should he reinjure the knee too soon.

"Well." She fumbled around on the desk, her back to him. Her voice had a funny catch in it. "That's great."

Holding the doctor's orders in one hand, she whipped around and smiled brightly. "That's terrific. Really, Jett.

I know how important this is to you. All your hard work has paid off."

He searched her face for some sign that she would miss him and found none. She looked bright, chipper, her cheeks slightly flushed with joy. She couldn't wait to see him gone.

"Another few days and I'm a free man again. Come December I'll be buckin' in Vegas."

"You must be ecstatic."

"Ecstatic doesn't begin to express how I feel."

Not even close. Because, instead of the release he'd expected, Jett experienced an undeniable sense of loss. If he left now, vibrant Becka would be at the mercy of boring Benchley. She'd probably wither up and die.

"Spend a minimum of thirty minutes in the whirlpool before workouts. The knee is a little stiff." She gathered her bag, slipped a purse over her shoulder.

Alarm shot through his nerve endings, every bit as uncomfortable as the soreness in his knee. He bit down on the inside of his lip to keep from asking her to stay.

After a struggle that frustrated him no end, he said, "Hey, Becka."

Stopping in the doorway, she looked over her shoulder. The movement emphasized the curve of her kissable lips and throat, and almost knocked the grin off his face.

"What?"

"Bingo's a dangerous game." Cocking a finger and thumb, he winked. "You crazy kids be careful out there."

For some reason Becka didn't crack a smile.

"Bingo was last night," she said, and shut the door behind her.

Jett growled at the closed door, then found his dart gun and took aim, pretending the bull's-eye was a certain stiff-necked insurance salesman.

Chapter Nine

Without looking back, Becka hurried down the hall-way and out into the yard. Every minute spent in Jett's company was killing her. His amused attitude about her dates was killing her. And the fact that he found her boring and pathetic was killing her. She had to stop this nonsense before doing something she'd regret forever.

Making her way around the side of the house to the carport, where her ancient Fairlane had been parked for weeks, she came to a decision. Driving Jett's truck was no longer a good idea. She wasn't here often enough to justify the need, and using anything of his only made her think about him more. Besides, he'd soon need the vehicle to return to his real life.

Swallowing back a moan of protest, she chastised herself for letting her relationship with him go beyond that of nurse and patient. Such a close friendship had no place in her profession.

Shaking her head in self-ridicule, Becka popped open the hood of her car.

Who was she kidding? Jett was more than a friend. For weeks, she'd fought the truth flowing like fresh springwater inside her, but the time had come to stop lying to herself. Jett was the man she wanted to be with, not Sherman.

And no matter how often she repeated her mantra that he was dangerous and unreliable, leaving him grew more and more difficult.

She, who'd vowed never to go near another reckless daredevil, feared the unthinkable—that she had fallen in love with Jett Garrett, king of the wild men. And if she let go of her fears, she'd want much more from Jett than he wanted to give.

Before anyone could discover her intentions, Becka filled the Fairlane's radiator with water, checked the tires and cranked the engine. Smoke and exhaust billowed as she drove away, leaving Jett and his truck behind. She should have been relieved. Instead, she ached with longing and regret for what could never be.

Twenty-five miles out of Rattlesnake, Becka met Kati's red SUV. Waving out the window to catch the sitter's attention, she pulled to the side of the sparsely traveled highway eager to see her son after a hard day.

As she approached Kati's parked vehicle, grasshoppers whirred through grass long dead from the scorching summer. Spotting his mother, Dylan unharnessed his car seat and barreled out the door before either adult could stop him.

"Mommy." Freckled nose wrinkled in joy, he darted toward her. Fear leaped into Becka's throat.

"Dylan. Get over here." She caught his arm and pulled him deeper into the grass. "Never, ever do that again. You could get run over. Do you hear me?"

Dylan stuck his thumb in his mouth and nodded, his burst of excitement gone in the wake of his mother's anxiety.

Holding tightly to her son's hand, Becka walked up to Kati's rolled-down window.

"Thanks for bringing him with you."

"Sorry he jumped out before I could stop him." Kati patted her rounded belly. "Baby Garrett has slowed me down a lot."

"It's not your fault, Kati. He knows better." She shook her head in dismay.

"He's coming out of his shell, and that can't be a bad thing."

Becka had her doubts about that. Her son had been fine until Jett interfered, insisting she allow Dylan the freedom to be his own person. Instead, he was becoming as frighteningly careless as the cowboy he hero-worshiped.

"I almost didn't recognize you in this car." Kati went on, leaning a slender elbow on the window. "Is Jett well enough to drive his truck again?"

"Almost. And since I'm not out here every day anymore, using his truck is neither necessary nor proper. My old car does fine around town."

"What does Jett have to say about that?"

"I didn't exactly tell him."

Kati narrowed her eyes in thought. "Becka, if I'm out of line here, please say so, but Jett's not in the habit of letting anyone drive that truck. The two of you seemed to have a grand time together. Even Colt mentioned the sparks. I'd thought—even hoped—there was something more than home health visits going on between the two of you."

Becka fought down a guilty blush. "Home health visits often get chummier than short-term arrangements in the hospital. That doesn't make them any less professional."

The reasoning was sound. However in this case it was a lie. She longed to be way more than chummy with this patient.

"Does a professional relationship extend to staying for supper every night, watching TV together, sitting on the patio long after dark?" She paused. "Kissing?"

Becka's head jerked up. "You saw us."

Kati's voice softened. She touched her friend's arm. "The two of you are so right for each other, Becka. Falling in love is a good thing."

"Love?" She tried to laugh it off. "Where did you get such a silly idea?"

"From the expression on your face when you look at Jett."

Becka went hot, then cold. Was she that obvious? So obvious that even Jett might have noticed?

"But I don't want to be in love with him."

"Becka! Why not? This is awesome. Jett needs a strong, solid woman like you, and I am tired of being the only female in a houseful of men. I'd adore having you for a sister-in-law."

Becka signaled a stop sign. "Wait a minute, Kati. Jett likes women. Regardless of my messed-up feelings, he's not interested in me beyond a little R & R.

This rehab period has bored him senseless. Naturally, he'd flirt with the one woman who came to his house every day."

"Jett isn't a man who spends much time with only one woman. If he'd wanted other females around, believe me, they would have been there. But within three days after you showed up at the ranch, the others disappeared. He even stopped taking their phone calls."

He had? Becka stared down at the shiny red car. Her own shocked reflection stared back as distorted as her emotions. Why had he done that?

With a shake of her head, she admitted the one thing that scared her most about falling for Jett. "Jett's too wild and restless for me. He'll get himself killed one of these days, and I don't want to be around to see it."

Kati studied her with sympathetic eyes. "Jett isn't Chris."

Becka flicked a grasshopper off her pant leg. "I wish people would stop saying that."

Kati arched her back. Her hugely pregnant belly bumped the steering wheel. "Did Jett ever tell you about his family? About how dysfunctional his parents were?"

"He mentioned his mother, that she wasn't exactly the homemaker type."

"Colt and Jett both suffered because of her self-centeredness. Not that the Garretts didn't provide well for their family. They did. But the kids never knew from one month to the next who their stepparents would be. From what Colt's told me, the fighting between their mom and dad didn't stop even after they divorced and remarried."

Becka couldn't imagine how this related to falling in love.

"That's a lousy way to bring up kids." Even though her mom had died from an aneurysm when she was eighteen, she'd had a normal, healthy upbringing. Oh, the family had their spats and she'd sparred with her brother until the day he joined the Marines, but as a family, they were solid as cement. And even though his health was bad, Dad was still there as moral support.

"I almost lost Colt," Kati went on. "Because I didn't understand that his fear of repeating his parents' mistakes held him at bay, not his lack of love for me."

"Jett doesn't care about anything that much."

Kati's soft smile lifted. "That's what he wants people to think."

What was Kati saying? That Jett's devil-may-care attitude was a protective shield to guard against emotional pain?

Dylan tugged at her arm. "Let's go, Mommy. I'm hungry."

Glad for the interruption, Becka released his hand. "Go on, then. Get in the car. I'll be there in a second."

The boy took off like a rocket. Becka returned her attention to Kati. "Gotta go, Kati. Thanks again for bringing Dylan this far."

"Anytime. And remember this." Squinting against the sunlight, she said, "If you love the man, don't let fear stand in the way. Fight for him. The Garrett men are worth it."

With Kati's words echoing in her head, Becka headed to her car. Instead of finding her son buckled up and ready, Dylan was outside, darting across the adjacent open field.

"Dylan," she called. "Let's go home."

The boy turned and waved, but didn't stop running in the opposite direction. "A rabbit, Mommy."

Becka sighed and started after him. They were going to be late. A stickler for schedules, Sherman hated to be kept waiting.

Calling her son's name, she loped across the pasture in pursuit. Seeing her coming, Dylan laughed and ran on. By the time she caught up to him, dust covered them both and she was angry. Though the weather had cooled, the days were still far too warm for running through an open field after a naughty child.

Was Sherman right? Should she discipline Dylan for every little misdemeanor? Or was Jett right? Was her constant emphasis on danger desensitizing Dylan so that he ignored her warnings even when they were most meaningful?

Scooping him into her arms, she carried him, kicking and twisting back to the car. If only kids came with instructions.

Once more she aimed the car toward town. Fifteen miles out of Rattlesnake her air conditioner quit. Nothing unusual, so she cranked down a window. The memory of Jett's cool, air-conditioned truck, scented with his aftershave tormented her.

Ten miles from town the car's temperature gauge climbed steadily higher until it reached the red zone. In her haste to leave the Garrett place, she hadn't refilled her water container.

"Come on, car, don't fail me now. Just a few more miles."

Five miles from Rattlesnake smoke seeped from beneath the hood like some evil genie. Amidst the hissing and boiling, the engine stuttered, then fell silent. Becka coaxed the tired old vehicle to the edge of the road, folded her arms on the steering wheel, put her head down and cried.

She cried for the dilapidated car. She cried because Dylan had disobeyed her. And she cried out of guilt because she didn't want to be with safe, predictable Sherman Benchley. Regardless of his lifestyle, regardless of how much he scared her, she loved Jett Garrett. And he had made it clear he was not the loving kind.

"Don't cry, Mommy." Dylan's small hand patted her shoulder as he slithered over the seat and cuddled up beside her. "It's okay. I love you."

Becka's spirit brightened a bit as her son repeated the comforting words she'd often said to him. Lifting her head, she pulled him into her arms, inhaled the sweaty-little-boy scent she adored and kissed his dark hair.

"I love you, too, baby, but our car won't run. We'll have to walk the rest of the way to town."

He batted innocent brown eyes at her. "We need a horse."

Becka couldn't hold back the laugh. Dabbing at her soupy eyes, she said, "If you're wishing, wish for a car."

"Okay." He screwed his eyes tight. "Magical, magical, I wish on a car."

Ah, if only life was that simple. Resigned to the five-mile walk, Becka shouldered the door open and helped Dylan out. Though five miles wasn't that far for someone in her physical condition, to a small child the distance would seem interminable. But what else could they do? Ranches in this part of Texas were miles apart with not a one in sight.

As they trudged along the dry, grassy shoulder of the road, a rare semi stopped to offer a ride, but Becka refused. As soon as the man roared off, leaving a cloud of fumes, she wished she'd asked him to call her dad when he reached Rattlesnake.

"Are we there yet, Mommy?" Dylan, who'd started off in a trot, now moved slower and slower. His upturned face was dabbled with sweat and dust, and Becka imagined her own looked the same. The child was wearing down fast.

"Want to ride piggyback for a while?" She squatted down, expecting him to climb aboard. Instead, he came around to face her.

"Don't mamas get tired?"

Tears stung the back of her eyes. For an ornery scamp, Dylan could be so thoughtful. "Never too tired for you. Climb on. Sherman is waiting to take us to supper."

As he wrapped his arms and legs around her back and neck, Dylan said. "I don't like him."

Hoisting him up, she stood and started off again. The straight, empty road seemed to go on forever with no town in sight. "Sherman's a nice man."

"He doesn't like me." Sweet, warm breath tickled her ear. "Jett likes me a big whole bunch."

Jett. Jett. Jett. Was there a conspiracy going on today? First Kati and now her own son forcing her to think about him in ways that were anything but healthy. Since she could think of little else, she didn't need their reminders.

"Jett will be leaving soon, son." Though his going was for the best, hearing the words spoken deepened her depression.

"I don't want him to go. I want him to be my daddy."

Becka thought her heart would stop for certain. The child had never experienced a relationship with his own father. She'd known the day would come when he'd realize what he'd missed, but she hadn't expected it so soon. Nor had she expected him to bond with someone like Jett.

Throat tight with regret and turmoil, she took off in a trot, effectively ending the unsettling conversation.

Thirty minutes later Dylan once again trudged wearily at her side. Arms aching, covered in sweat and dust, Becka was too thirsty to think about Jett or Sherman or anything else except getting home.

Behind her came the sound of an approaching vehicle. Grabbing Dylan, she moved farther away from the road to let the driver pass safely. Instead a familiar silver-and-blue truck rumbled to a stop alongside them.

Jett, leaning across the seat, pushed the door open. "I don't suppose you strangers would like a ride."

Suddenly reenergized, Dylan catapulted toward the truck, grabbed Jett's hand and was hauled into the cab. "I knew you would come. Where's your horse?"

Jett looked to Becka, one eyebrow a question mark. Wearily she waved him off. "Don't ask me to explain four-year-old logic."

Leaning around the boy, Jett offered her his hand. Though armed with his charming grin, his blue eyes rested on her, serious and concerned.

"Glad to see me?"

Placing her palm in his, Becka felt safe and protected—which made no sense at all given her rescuer. Her heart thudded as he hauled her into the truck. Glad to see him? He couldn't begin to guess.

To sidestep the loaded question, she said. "What made you come?"

"Kati." Sliding the shifter into first, Jett set the truck into motion. "When she told me you'd taken your car, I got a real bad feeling and figured I should check it out."

Grateful, Becka said, "Dylan was nearly done in." So was she.

Dylan, riding between the two adults, gazed up at Jett with adoration. "My feets got tired."

Jett tapped him on the nose. "Your face is dirty."

"So's Mommy's."

Jett shifted his gaze from the road to her and back again. "Yep. Sure is."

The tingle generated only by Jett shimmied down her tired body. She pressed back against the seat to stop that nonsense. "I'm so thirsty, I don't care."

He thumped the steering wheel with the palm of his hand. "I know the cure for that. Cherry limeade coming right up."

With single-minded cheerfulness, he drove the last couple of miles into town, keeping up a witty chatter.

Kati's words played through Becka's head as she soaked in Jett's vibrant personality. She enjoyed looking at his dark, handsome face and dancing blue eyes. She liked listening to the rich timbre of his laughter. And she loved the way he made her feel like a woman.

He'd be gone soon, pursuing the one prize that captivated him far more than she ever could. But today she could look her fill and let her heart love him. And he would never have to know.

Pulling into the town's only drive-in restaurant, Jett pushed the button on the outside speakers and ordered three cherry limeades. When the clerk asked if he wanted anything else, Jett glanced over his shoulder and asked, "Anyone for a chili dog?"

"Me, me," Dylan cried, raising up on his knees to look out the window.

Becka glanced at her watch, saw the time was well past the appointed six-thirty and groaned. Wishing she could spend a few more hours with Jett, she forced out a refusal. "Sorry, baby. No time. Sherman is already waiting for us."

Jett's rolled his eyes heavenward, then spoke into the speaker. "That's all, thanks."

When the drinks arrived, Becka and Dylan eagerly gulped down the icy, tart refreshment while Jett backed out and headed toward her house.

As they turned the corner onto her quiet, residential street, Becka saw that Sherman had, indeed, arrived. He sat on her sunny front porch, back straight, glaring with annoyance when Becka climbed out of Jett's truck.

Rising, he came to the curb to meet her, his attention riveted on the fountain drinks she and Dylan carried. "So this is what took you so long."

"Not really."

But he didn't wait for her explanation. "I don't appreciate being kept waiting while you're having drinks with another man."

"Drinks? This is a cherry limeade." What had come over her usually calm, passionless friend? "Jett happened to do me a favor. You have no reason to be upset."

Behind her, she heard the driver's side door open and felt, more than saw, Jett come up the slight rise from the street.

"Benchley." Jett's voice was cordial, but tension radiated off him like sun off a metal roof. "I think you should let the lady explain."

"All right." Glaring at his watch, Sherman tilted his head. "We've already missed our dinner reservation, anyway."

Becka held back an annoyed retort. Is that all that mattered to him?

"My car broke down about five miles out of town."

"I thought you were driving *his* truck."

"No. I was driving my own car." What she drove was her business, not his, and she had no intention of explaining.

"And Garrett just happened to come along at the perfect time to give you a ride?" His lips pressed in a disapproving line.

"As a matter of fact, yes. He realized I might have trouble in that dilapidated excuse for a car."

A slow dawning, like daybreak after a stormy night, filtered into her consciousness. Sherman had sat here on her porch, waiting with annoyance when he knew she should have been home by now. He hadn't worried that something had happened because he was too busy fretting over his dinner reservation.

Jett, on the other hand, had gotten into his vehicle and come looking for her.

The heat that had been embarrassment turned to anger, not at Sherman, but at herself. She'd misjudged him, thinking his rigidity and control meant protection and safety.

"Sherman." She placed a hand on his arm to gentle the words, fighting off the inevitable guilt. Her con-

fused feelings were not Sherman's fault. He'd filled a
need in her life, but she didn't love him, and dating was
wrong for both of them. "You've been kind to Dylan and
me, but we're not going out to dinner tonight or any
other night."

"I should have known this was coming. You're giving up on us because of him." He cast a hostile glare toward Jett.

"There is no *us,* Sherman. And I'm sorry if I led you
to think there could be. But you've been a good friend
for a long time, and that means a lot to me. Please say
that won't change."

Emotions shifted across the salesman's face—confusion, relief and finally acceptance.

"All right, then. I guess Mother was right." With a last
resentful glance at Jett, he stepped around Becka and got
as far as his car before turning back. "You will be keeping your policies with me?"

If the question hadn't been so pathetic, she'd have
laughed. "I'd be crazy not to." And maybe she was
crazy, anyway. "You've taken wonderful care of my insurance needs."

Becka watched him drive away. Though guilt wanted
to consume her, she'd done the right thing. Maybe her
timing had been bad with Jett here listening, but she'd
been honest with Sherman and with herself. And the
truth felt good.

Taking a final slurp at her now-empty cup, her glance
slid toward Jett. Some truths were better kept to herself.

Drawing in a deep cleansing breath, she accepted the
fact that she loved Jett Garrett. Without him to shake her
out of her lethargy, she might one day have drifted into

a bloodless marriage with a man she didn't love. If anything, she owed Jett for making her realize she needed passion…and she needed love. Settling for less cheated all concerned.

But he was still that dangerous man, that maniac bull rider, and he was still preparing to leave. Love—hers, at least—wouldn't change that.

"Thanks for the ride home, Jett."

"No problem." Eyes dancing, he rubbed his hands together. "So now can we go back and get those chili dogs?"

She had already lost her heart and maybe her mind. What possible harm would there be in enjoying the little time she could with the man she loved?

Tossing her cup into the Dumpster at the curb, she admitted, "A chili dog sounds great," and climbed back into Jett's truck.

Chapter Ten

Jett's breath caught in his lungs.

He'd never seen Becka in anything but scrubs or sweats or shorts, but now she stood at her front door in a dress—a royal-blue dress that set her hair aflame and glided over her curves like heated suntan oil. She'd done something to her hair, too, so that it hung in full gentle waves to her shoulders. His gaze slithered down her body to where a length of shapely leg ended in a strappy, sexy pair of shoes.

He'd never been speechless in his life, but right now he couldn't say anything except "Wow."

How could a simple dress and a pair of shoes be so blamed sexy? He was practically salivating.

Becka performed a sassy, smiling curtsy. "Why, thank you, cowboy. You look pretty good yourself."

He glanced down at his purple shirt and tie, glad

he'd spiffed up for their car-buying trip to Amarillo. Cookie, when he'd discovered Jett's outing involved Becka, had even creased his best jeans and steamed his new Resistol. But a new hat and a little starch couldn't hold a candle to beautiful Becka.

"The car salesman will take one look at you and *give* you a car."

"Here's hoping." She slid a tiny purse onto her shoulder, turned the lock in the door and started to his truck. Wicked man that he was, he lagged behind to watch her walk and was well rewarded for his efforts.

Since two days ago when she'd given boring Benchley the kiss-off—a moment that would live happily in his memory forever—she'd loosened up and agreed to hang out with him some. Actually, he'd hounded her into spending every spare minute in his company. And she didn't seem to mind at all.

Yep. Life was looking up.

Becka was a woman of passion whether she knew it or not, and Benchley was about as passionate as a chastity belt. Jett was glad she figured out that Mr. Rigor-Mortis wasn't her type.

A woman as special as Becka deserved better. She deserved a man like… Rounding the front of the Silverado, he paused. He couldn't actually think of a man good enough for Becka. In fact, the idea of Becka with someone else set his teeth on edge. Best not to think about that on such a great day as this.

Opening the passenger side door, he couldn't resist sliding his hands around Becka's waist and boosting her into the tall truck cab. Trouble was, once she settled into the seat, he had a hard time letting go. She looked at him with those honey-colored eyes alight and happy, and he wanted to body-slam her onto the bench seat and hop aboard.

He sucked in a lungful of her perfume and backed away. Maybe later. First they had a car to buy.

When she'd expressed her plans to purchase another used car, he'd insisted on going with her. He wanted to leave Rattlesnake knowing Becka had safe, dependable transportation. Not that he was in the habit of worrying about women, but Becka was different somehow. She'd saved his career. He owed her.

A bull rider couldn't afford to have distractions weighing on his mind. Becka and her car situation were definitely distractions. Today he'd solve this one last problem so he could leave for Santa Fe this weekend with a clear head.

"Dylan okay with staying behind?" he asked as he put the truck into gear.

"Dad promised him ice cream and a romp in the park."

"And I promised to bring him a toy truck from Amarillo."

"Did you?" Thankfully, she looked pleased.

Lifting one shoulder, he slid a CD into the player. A rocky country tune filled the truck's interior. "Dylan's my man."

"He feels the same way about you."

"Yeah, I know." And the knowing filled him with a kind of satisfaction he hadn't experienced before. Too bad he wouldn't see the kid for a while. The little critter had gotten under his skin. "I noticed you've eased up on him a little."

"I still worry about him, but I'm trying to let him grow."

"That's normal, isn't it? For a parent to worry some?" Not that he'd know anything about normal parents. "As long as you don't worry to the point of scaring the kid to death."

"Which I do."

"Aw, don't beat yourself up. He's a great kid." He slid his gaze sideways then quickly realized that was not a good idea. Becka's straight skirt had crept up a few inches, and though she remained modestly covered, his imagination went berserk.

Swallowing a knot the size of Houston, he said, "After we find a killer deal on a car, how about a Mexican dinner at Amigo's?"

"An offer I can't refuse. I love Mexican food." In rhythm with the music, she tapped her fingertips against her leg.

Jett itched to feel that smooth skin beneath his own hand. Sweat popped out beneath his collar. He hummed along with the music, but his gaze kept straying to Becka, to lips he wanted to kiss and skin he wanted to touch.

Finally, he gave up and reached for her hand. He had to touch her. Letting his fingers rest for a second or two against her silky leg, he pulled her hand against his thigh and held it there.

Without protest, Becka studied him for a moment before those luscious lips curved upward. His heart went airborne like the time he'd gone cliff diving in Mexico. He didn't know what ailed him lately, but his insides went haywire every time she looked at him. Another reason he opted for the trip to Amarillo. An entire day spent shopping with a woman always left him happy to be a bachelor. By day's end, he'd be tired of Becka and ready to move on.

And that's exactly the way he wanted it.

Two days later Becka found herself walking along the lakeshore beside Jett. She didn't know how he'd convinced her to come here, but during the last week he'd talked her into a lot things. He'd helped her buy a car, haggling the salesman down to far less money than she'd expected to pay. Then after dinner, he'd taken her dancing. Even though his knee was still in a brace and she'd nagged him to take it easy, they'd had a blast. She'd laughed so much, she'd wanted the day to never end. And when he'd pulled her into his arms for one last slow dance, and she'd pressed her cheek to his wonderful, manly chest, her heart had soared on wings of love.

Now here they were in the very place where her whole life had changed in an instant. She hadn't been here since that awful day four years ago, but Jett was right. The time had come to face her ghosts and let them go. Hiding from her guilt and from the things she loved—and who she was—served no good purpose. Hadn't she proven as much by dating Sherman when they were not suited? Honesty—especially with oneself—was a good thing.

The leaves on the few cottonwood trees surrounding the lake had turned silver, and the blue-gray water lapped softly against the banks. Only a handful of diehards were out here this late in the season, for which Becka was thankful.

As they walked around the water's edge, Dylan, beneath Becka's watchful eye, skipped happily along ahead of them, unaware of the tragedy that had befallen him on this spot. She let the child play, no longer quite so terrified of unseen dangers—another thing Jett had helped her through. Filling Dylan with fears and restrictions would damage him. Letting go wasn't easy, but she was determined to try.

They walked along for a time before either of them spoke. She thought of Chris, of his exuberant life, his tragic death, and slowly the guilt and horror of that day eased, drifting out with the gentle tide.

Tilting her head back she gazed upward into the heavens and let go. A bird, too far away to identify, winged overhead, and she watched until it disappeared in the smattering of wispy white clouds.

Feeling Jett's anxious gaze, she turned her attention to him. Hatless, in a navy western shirt and blue jeans with the walking splint secured around his knee, he stole her breath. His warm hand closed over hers, and the action seemed so natural she didn't resist.

"You okay?"

A breeze ruffled her hair, but Jett ruffled her heart. She hadn't expected this sweet concern from him.

She nodded. "Coming here has helped me somehow, though I can't explain it."

"No need to. That's what I'd hoped."

"I thought I'd be sad, and maybe I am a little, but I also remember the fun Chris had here. The way he loved the water. If he'd known he was going to die, he would have chosen here."

"I understand that."

She studied him. "Yes. I think you do."

Stopping to pick up a pebble, she sailed it out across

the water. "I've missed this place. Missed swimming and skiing and boating."

"No reason not to start up again."

"Maybe." She slipped her hand back into his, needing his strength.

"Tell you what. Next summer this knee will be good as new. Sometime when I'm back this way, we'll come out here and ski together. What do you say?"

If he'd chipped her heart with a pick ax, she wouldn't have felt any sharper pain than the one tearing through her now. "Sure."

"Good. It's a date then." He looked inordinately happy while her heart ripped in two. Watching him leave, now that she'd risked loving him, wouldn't be easy. She worried about him being injured again—maybe even killed—and the thought nearly brought her to her knees.

"Jett, I—" she hesitated, longing to share her beautiful secret, but not sure he wanted to hear it. "I want to tell you something."

Pulling her around to face him, he said, "Shoot."

"I—" The words wouldn't come, those three little words that screamed to be said.

He looked at her quizzically, pulling her close enough that she saw the tiny lines around his eyes. She loved those lines. She loved the bump where his nose had been broken in football. And she loved him. But telling him would ruin their friendship and drive him away forever.

Finally she settled for an easier truth. "You're a pretty nice guy under all that machismo."

He grinned. "Shh. Don't tell anybody. You'll ruin my rep."

"Your secret is safe with me."

"I knew I could trust you, Becka-Rebecka." Eyes smiling, he came closer, studied her for a long, questioning moment while her heart thudded painfully. And then his mouth covered hers in a kiss that melted her bones and sent her soaring.

When the kiss ended, he asked, "Ever been to Santa Fe?"

Nerve endings abuzz, she pulled back, surprised. "Why?"

Still holding one of her hands, he hitched a shoulder. "I'm heading down there day after tomorrow. Maybe Dylan could stay with Kati or his grandpa for a couple of days while you go with me. I'd like knowing you're in the stands when I take my first bull ride."

"Why? So you'd have a nurse handy." She tried to joke, but the idea that he was nearing departure took the fun out of everything.

He stared down at her for the longest moment, his eyes telegraphing why he wanted her in Santa Fe. "No. Not as a nurse."

She knew what he asked. To spend a weekend alone—no strings attached—to explore this passion singing between them. And Becka wanted to go more than she wanted her next breath. But after that one satisfying weekend, Jett would be gone again, and she would come home alone with a wounded heart. A weekend with Jett would never be enough.

"Not a good idea."

"I thought it was." Hands on her waist, he pulled her to him again and his lips found hers—sweet and hot and persuasive. Becka kissed him back with all the love and sorrow welling inside her.

When she was at the point of surrender, of agreeing to spend the weekend in his arms, Dylan insinuated his small form between them, breaking them apart.

Face tilted upward, he said to Jett, "Are you gonna marry my mom?"

"Dylan!" Taking her opportunity to escape, she slipped to her knees in front of her son. Her cheeks flooded with heat. "What made you say such a thing?"

Dylan's lip quivered. "Evan said if you kissed, maybe you'd get married. And Jett could be my daddy."

"Oh, baby." She hugged him to her. The scent of fresh air and dirty hands assailed her. "Jett is leaving on Saturday. Kissing me won't make him your daddy." If it would, her heart wouldn't be breaking in two.

Jett's hand came down to stroke Dylan's hair, but he offered no ready quip.

"But you know what?" She tried to cheer her son, as well as herself. "Next summer, Jett's coming back and he'll bring us out here. Maybe you can even go swimming." She had never let him near the water but the time had come. A child needed to learn water safety just as she needed to live again—without Jett.

"Really?" He perked up, gazing at his hero with adoring brown eyes.

Jett nodded. "You bet."

"Cool." Dylan ducked away, started to suck his thumb, but shoved the hand in his pocket instead. Becka's heart nearly burst with pride.

Using Jett's offered hand for leverage, she rose and dusted the sand from her knees. "Sorry about that." She gave a little shrug. "Kids."

"Yeah." He shook his head but didn't smile. "Kids."

"I think we should go now. Come on, Dylan."

By mutual consent they started for the truck, but she didn't take Jett's hand again.

Dylan's innocent question had broken the spell between them and kept her from making a regrettable mistake. But would she still feel that way when the man she loved drove away and didn't look back?

Chapter Eleven

Coming through the industrial-size kitchen of the Garrett Ranch, Jett snitched a handful of chocolate chip cookies and listened to Cookie's usual bluster before chuckling off down the hall.

As he headed to the den, he whistled. Then he sang, ripping off a cheerful version of "Zipadee-do-da," because today was indeed a wonderful day.

He'd ridden Skipper for an hour with only a tinge of pain and some residual soreness from the Amarillo trip. Nothing he couldn't live with. And the flexible brace around his knee allowed him plenty of movement.

Becka had chewed on him good for dancing too much and making the knee swell. Funny how her nagging had made him happy instead of mad.

He flexed his arms, executed a one-legged knee bend,

sucked in his flat, six-pack belly. He was in great shape, thanks to Becka-Rebecka, and ready to rock and roll.

He'd even paid his entry fee to the rodeo in Santa Fe. If only he could convince Becka to go with him, life would be perfect. He knew she wanted to, but for some reason she held back.

Grabbing a couple of dumbbells, he executed ten quick arm curls.

Removing the brace from his knee, Jett slipped his leg into the passive motion machine and turned it on. Though he was using the machine less all the time, every bit of exercise brought him closer to perfect health.

Outside he heard the sounds of childish laughter as Evan and Dylan played tag in the backyard. An hour ago Kati had arrived with Dylan in tow, announcing that Becka was working late at the hospital. Knowing he'd see Becka before the night was over, Jett had been both delighted and invigorated, a reaction he didn't examine too closely.

Hey, Becka was a cool lady and they had fun together. End of subject. Just because he liked her more than the other ladies he'd known, didn't mean diddly. Tonight was the last night he'd be in Rattlesnake, so why not spend it with her?

While the machine hummed and flexed his knee, Jett hefted the dumbbells over his head and worked his triceps. He'd just completed twenty-five reps when he heard Kati cry out.

Lowering the weights, he shut off the machine and listened, She called out again, her voice edged in anxiety, rising slightly. This time he made out the words.

"Boys, come back here."

His pulse kick-started. Something was up. Kati never panicked.

In less time than he took to make the buzzer on a bull ride, Jett was out of the machine, down the hall, and out the back door.

At first he saw only Kati, moving toward the open pasture with all the speed of a terrapin, her advanced state of pregnancy no match for two fleet-footed four-year-olds. As he scanned the horizon, following Kati's frantic pointing, he saw the two boys in the distance. Evan and Dylan had scooted under the five-strand barb-wire fence and were chasing each other across the field and farther away from the house.

He cupped his mouth with his hands and bellowed, "Evan. Dylan."

He held his breath, listening. Neither turned to answer, and he realized they'd gone too far to hear his call.

Moving at a fast clip, Jett caught up to Kati. She stood at the fence, breathless, both hands supporting her belly. Strain pulled at her usually tranquil face.

"They were playing along the fence and before I realized it, they were halfway across the field."

"No need to panic. They'll be okay."

"But they'll get lost if they go into that tree line."

Jett didn't want to think of the dangers among those trees, but he saw his concern reflected in Kati's eyes. The woods surrounded a deep, rocky ravine that supported a small stream of water. When running, as it was now, that stream fed into the stock pond. All provided potential hazards to a small child.

His pulse kicked up another notch, but he kept his

cool. Kati was feeling guilty enough without him freaking.

He stretched the fence wires apart and slid through them. "I'll have them back here in no time."

She started to protest. "But your knee—"

"Right as the mail." He wished he'd had time to don the brace. Rushing this far had already set his knee to throbbing.

Ignoring the ache, he hurried across the pasture and headed straight toward the ravine. The boys were out of sight, but occasionally faint voices drifted back to him.

Fifty yards from the tree line, he flushed a covey of quail and the sudden flight of a dozen birds startled him. He paused to look around. When he caught sight of Evan's dark head bobbing toward him through the tall grass, he suffered an undeniable adrenaline surge.

"Where's Dylan?" he asked, yanking the boy into his embrace.

Evan, unaware he'd caused a fright, pointed toward the trees. "Down there. He fell."

Nothing much scared Jett, but those words sent a shaft of terror through him. What had happened to Becka's boy?

A quick glance toward the house told him Kati was following, though she was far behind. He hoisted Evan into the air and waved then set the child on his feet, heading him toward his mother.

Picking up speed, he all but ran to the ravine, stopping occasionally to call Dylan's name.

Though the area was more rock than anything, a scramble of brush and low-hanging grapevines impeded his progress. He saw no sign of Dylan.

Reaching the ravine, he rushed along the edge, peering down, hoping the boy hadn't fallen onto the sharp rocky surface below.

"Dylan." His cry was answered only by a hawk.

A little farther down, near the stream's edge he spotted something purple. Moving to the ledge, he lay on his stomach and peered over the side. A height this dangerous always got his adrenaline pumping, but this time wasn't fun.

Dylan lay crumpled at the bottom of a twenty-foot ravine, one tennis-shoe-clad foot trailing in the water.

While Jett rested there, pondering his choices, the noise of someone moving through the brush drew his attention. Swiveling, he sat up as Kati came into sight.

"Did you find him?" Her face was pinched and white.

"Yeah. He's down there."

Rushing to the edge, Kati gazed down and gasped. "Oh, Jett. He's so still."

Jett didn't want to think about that. Keeping his voice cool and steady, he ordered, "Go back to the house. Call 911. I'll take care of him."

Her eyes widened. "You're not going down there?"

"I have to." Grimly, he thought of the choices. There were none. Colt was in Austin. He had no idea where any of the hands were. And Cookie was in no shape to rappel down the side of a recliner, much less a twenty-foot ravine. He wasn't, either, come to think of it, but that didn't matter. Dylan was hurt. Maybe even… Jett refused to let his thoughts go there. If he had to, he'd crawl down those rocks buck naked. One way or another, he'd bring Dylan up to safety.

"How? How can you get to him without falling yourself?"

He looked around, thinking, searching for something to hang on to as he made the steep descent. His gaze fell to the oversize grapevines hanging from the trees, but he didn't share his thought with Kati. Who knew if such a thing would hold his weight? "I'll think of something. Now go. And hurry."

As soon as she and Evan disappeared through the trees, Jett searched for the largest vine. He'd swung on vines like these as a kid. Though they grew up out of the ground, they crawled up tree branches and grew so long they hung down. At least three inches thick and flexible, they'd been great for an eighty-pound kid. But would they hold a grown man?

Finding the thickest ground root, Jett followed it up into the tree then yanked hard, unraveling the vine until he had a length of at least twenty feet. Gripping it with both hands, he leaned back with all his weight, testing the vine's strength. It held.

He tossed his makeshift rope over the edge of the ravine, turned with his face to the wall, muttered, "Piece of cake," and started down.

He'd done some rappelling, descending the steep inclines at Red Rock Canyon, and knew the technique. Pushing out with his good leg, he edged backward, letting his hands slide down the vine as his body lowered several feet.

A stab of pain ripped into his knee as he made contact with the ravine wall. The idea flickered through his head that he shouldn't be doing this. His knee wasn't ready. He should wait for help.

From below came a childish whimper. Jett's determination soared. Injured knee or not, he had to get to Dylan.

Becka would be devastated if anything happened to her son.

So would he.

He pushed off again, felt the crunch and tear deep in his leg. Sweat popped out all over his body. He gritted his teeth.

Becka. Dylan. He couldn't let them down.

Rocks jutted out, jabbing into him. He pushed off again. Pushing off wasn't bad, but the inevitable return, the moment when his feet rammed into the cliff's edge, was pure torment.

Halfway down, he knew the end result for his body would not be pretty. He was destroying his knee and with it, all dreams of the NFR.

Then truth slammed into him as powerful as the pain. He recognized what he'd been denying for weeks. Nothing and no one was as important as Dylan and Becka. Not the NFR. Not even his own body.

He loved them. He needed them in his life more than breath. And he'd die on these rocks before he'd let either of them be hurt in any way. With a strength he didn't think possible, he blocked the explosive pain and concentrated on rescuing Becka's son—the child he wanted for his own.

He, Jett Garrett, who wasn't afraid of anything, was terrified of losing the two people who'd come to mean more to him than anything.

By the time he reached the bottom, his left leg was a wobbling mess of useless agony. Still, he managed to drag himself to the child's side.

"Dylan. Son, can you hear me?" He touched the child's small shoulder, afraid to turn him over and afraid not to.

"Jett?" a small, frightened voice whimpered. "Jett."

"Where are you hurt?" He ran his hands over the sobbing boy, gently lifting and searching until he was satisfied that no bones were broken. Carefully he rolled Dylan onto his back. As soon as the child saw his rescuer, he bounded up from the rocky ground and into Jett's arms.

Jett sat there holding Dylan, debating a climb back up when he heard the distant scream of a siren. The ambulance had made good time.

Rocking Becka's boy and singing the Barney song, he waited, the oddest emotion filling his chest like a helium balloon. He hurt like a son of a gun, he was stuck in a ravine with a crying child and he'd just given up his dreams of glory.

But he also had discovered what it meant to really love somebody.

And he felt like a king.

Becka was a basket case.

In a hospital as small as Rattlesnake Municipal, the two ambulances were housed in an adjoining annex. The hospital staff knew every time one was called out and received radio updates about the estimated time of arrival, the patient and the type of injury.

When she'd heard the ambulance's destination and later that the patient was a child, every latent fear had exploded. Dylan was at the Garrett Ranch.

Thinking the worst, she paced the hallway, waiting, peering out the glass doors over and over until she thought she would go mad from the uncertainty.

"Becka." One of the orderlies clapped a compassionate hand on her shoulder. "Why don't you take a break?"

She shook her head, holding back a scream. "They'll be here any minute."

Sure enough, within seconds the waning wail of a siren announced the ambulance's arrival.

Barreling through the double doors, Becka met the paramedics as they lowered the stretcher to the ground. A small figure with sticks and leaves in his brown hair lay on the gurney, his eyes closed.

"Oh, no!" Becka's knees threatened to give way. "Please, oh, please. Not Dylan, too."

He was so still.

She grabbed the paramedic's arm. "How bad is he? Somebody tell me."

"You'll need to ask the doctor." And he rolled past her, making the turn into an exam room.

Becka followed, fighting a rising hysteria. What had happened to her baby?

Her worst nightmare had come to pass and she was responsible. She'd let Dylan out of her sight and something horrible had occurred. He was injured. Regardless of what Jett and everyone else said, she never should have let down her guard.

She charged into the room, shaking all over. At the sight of her son lying on the exam table, a sob broke from her throat. The doctor on call took one look at her and pointed. "Out."

Becka knew he was right. Hysterical mothers, even nurses, had no business in the emergency room. Hadn't she escorted a number of them into the lobby herself?

The thought no more than crossed her mind when one of the other nurses slipped an arm through hers and guided her into the hall. "I'll let you know something as soon as we check him over."

The pneumatic door sucked closed, blocking her view of her baby boy. Becka leaned her back against the cool block wall, closed her eyes and tried to slow the pounding of her heart. If she lost Dylan, she hoped her heart stopped completely.

"Becka." At the familiar voice her eyes flew open.

Against the opposite wall, Jett sat in one of the wheelchairs kept there for incoming patients.

Why was Jett with Dylan? What was he doing here unless…? Suddenly a hideous suspicion flashed into her mind.

Half-insane with terror and guilt, she erupted, flying at him. "I should have known you would be involved. What did you do to my baby?"

An odd expression on his face, he reached out as if to touch her. "Becka."

She shrank back, trembling with rage. "Don't touch me. Don't you dare."

His hand fell to his lap. "Sweetheart, listen."

"Don't you sweetheart me." Out of her head with terror, she clenched her fists at her side and loomed over him. "Don't you dare try to use your charm and wit to get out of this. This time your irresponsible behavior hurt someone other than yourself. You've injured an innocent child. A child who adores you, who would do anything to impress you."

She railed at him, letting loose all the pent-up anxiety and tension of the last half hour.

He said nothing. Pale and stony-faced, his blue eyes never wavered. His silence only added fuel to her fire.

"What did you do? Dare him to ride a motorcycle? Ask him to *trust you* to catch him while he jumped from the barn roof?" Knowing he hated such action, she poked a finger into his chest. "'Trust me,' you said. And like a fool I did. I believed you when you said you weren't like Chris. I believed you when you said you'd never let anything happen to Dylan and me. You even made me believe I was too protective of him. And now look what's happened."

What an idiot she'd been to let herself fall in love with another thoughtless, self-centered man. Her sweet baby son had suffered because she was blinded by her love for Jett.

The door behind them opened. "Becka, you can come in now." Marla turned her attention to Jett. "Mr. Garrett, you doing okay? I'll take you to exam room two in just a minute."

Becka looked from the nurse to Jett, thinking Marla must be mistaken. Dylan was injured. Not Jett. But she had no time to clear up the confusion with the other nurse. Dylan waited.

Whirling, she charged into the room, leaving Jett to wallow in his own guilt.

"He's fine, Becka," the doctor said, smiling down at Dylan who now sat on the side of the table, dirty legs dangling over the sides.

"A few bruises and scratches and a twisted ankle. I've ordered an X-ray, to be certain, but I don't think we'll find a thing to worry about."

Relief, warm and cleansing as a hot bath, flooded her as she slid onto the table and hugged Dylan to her. "But he was so still in the ambulance."

Dr. Clayton smiled. "That's because he was asleep."

Dylan looked up her. "Jett sing'd to me and I got sleepy."

Becka stiffened. She didn't want to feel gratitude to Jett. He'd been the cause of the accident in the first place.

"The tech will take Dylan down to X-ray soon. I need to check Mr. Garrett's injuries right now, but I'll talk to you again in a bit."

As the doctor exited the room Becka sat there baffled. Jett was hurt? How?

The image of him in the wheelchair came to mind. She'd thought he was behaving in his usual cavalier manner, taking a rest in the only available seat. Her frantic mind had barely registered the Ace bandage or the fact that he'd been slumped forward, both hands wrapped around his knee.

One of the paramedics came into the room. "Your boy okay?"

"Yes. Nothing serious, thank goodness." Her pulse had finally fallen below danger level, but the adrenaline rush left her weak.

"Lucky for him Jett Garrett's got a daredevil streak."

She blinked at him, more baffled than ever. What was going on? "I don't understand."

"Didn't Garrett tell you what happened?"

She hadn't given him a chance. Dread replaced her fear. "No."

"Dylan fell into that ravine down in the Garrett pasture. Jett rappelled down after him." His expression bespoke both admiration and regret. "I think he may have screwed up his leg pretty bad in the process."

For a split second Becka's heart stuttered to a standstill. Jett had harmed himself to save Dylan. The risk-taking trait she'd feared so much had been the very thing that had rescued her son.

A tidal wave of realization swept over her. All her control, all her safety precautions hadn't helped Dylan, but Jett's courage to take a chance had.

She pressed her hand against her mouth to keep from crying. "Oh, Jett. What have you done? What have I done?"

At that moment Kati and Evan swept into the room. Kati's face was pinched and white. "Is Dylan okay?"

She rushed to the little patient and began to sob, her serenity lost in concern. "I'm so sorry Becka. This was all my fault. Dylan wouldn't come back when I called him, and I was too slow and pregnant to catch him before…before—"

Becka laid a reassuring hand on her friend's arm. She couldn't blame Kati. Hadn't Dylan run away from her a dozen times lately? "Kati, he's going to be fine, I promise. But Jett…"

Becka couldn't bear to think of the ugly words she'd said to the man she claimed to love.

Dylan, beginning to bask in the attention, sat up straighter and took his thumb from his mouth. "I hurt my knee like Jett."

Taking a tissue from the open box on the counter, Kati wiped her soggy face. "How is Jett? His knee looked awful when they brought him out of that ravine."

Becka closed her eyes briefly. "Oh, Kati, I've made a horrible mistake. I didn't know he'd hurt himself trying to save Dylan. I accused him of causing the accident."

Dylan's freckled face turned up to her. "Jett loves me, Mommy. He wouldn't hurt me. When I was scared, he held me and told me. And he sing'd, too. I like it when Jett sings."

Becka liked it, too. She loved it. And she loved him.

"He's hurt pretty bad, Becka. When they brought him up out of that ravine, he couldn't use his left leg at all. But he hopped to the ambulance and blew it off as if his leg weren't dangling uselessly. All he cared about was Dylan. He kept saying you'd trusted him and he couldn't let anything happen to his boy." She pinned Becka with a hard gaze. "He loves you, Becka. He may not know it yet, but he does. Go find him and tell him the truth before it's too late."

Pain and regret crashed into Becka with the force of an eighteen-wheeler. "He'd never believe me now."

"Then make him believe you. He's worth it." She gave Becka a gentle push. "Go. I'll stay with Dylan."

Drawing on all her courage, Becka slid from the table. She kissed Dylan on the forehead. "Be back in a minute, sweetie."

Even if he turned her away she had to tell him. He deserved to know he was a hero in her eyes.

Chapter Twelve

Becka poked her head into three rooms before she found him. Alone, sitting on an exam table in his boxers, he lifted his head when she opened the door. For a millisecond his eyes lit up, but almost immediately he averted his gaze.

"Jett." How did she apologize for so gross an error? And how did she tell him the most important thing of all? "Please look at me. I have something to tell you."

Immediately he met her eyes. "Is Dylan all right?"

Another chink fell from her already battered heart. His concern was only for Dylan, not himself, though his was far the more serious of the injuries. "He'll be fine. A twisted ankle, a skinned knee."

Closing his eyes, he blew out a relieved sigh. "Thank goodness."

Hesitantly she came deeper into the room. "I'm so sorry. I didn't know."

He shook his head. Bits of leaves stuck to his hair. "Forget it. No matter what I say or do, you'll never trust me."

Her chest ached from knowing what he'd sacrificed.

"You're wrong. You gave up your dreams to save my son. I can never repay that."

Jaw tight, he said, "I didn't do it for pay."

"I know. You went down that ravine after my son because you're a man of courage, a man who takes action when other people stand around and wonder what to do." Swallowing the welling tears, she whispered. "You're a hero, Jett. My hero."

Wary eyes watched as she approached the exam table. "When Chris died I felt so responsible, and I thought by avoiding all the activities I loved, all the things that made my blood race and my heart pump with excitement that I would be safe, that I would never have to live through that kind of trauma again. Then you came along and threw me off balance. *You* made my blood race. *You* made my heart pump with excitement. You scared me out of my safe, boring, miserable shell."

"Sorry."

"No, silly. Don't you get it? You've helped me understand that life lived in fear isn't life at all. It's existence. I want more than that. And I want my son to have more than that, too."

"Good. He deserves more."

"I know you don't want to hear this, but I'm going to tell you anyway."

Heart in her throat, she took his hand. To her relief, he didn't pull away.

She drew in a deep breath, held it as she gathered her

courage—courage Jett had helped her find again. "I love you, Jett."

Astonishment flooding his face, he opened his mouth to speak.

Becka stopped him. "No, let me say this. I know you're not the settling-down kind. I know you're not interested in a permanent relationship, but I want to be with you as long as you want me, however you want me. If you could still go to Santa Fe, I'd go with you. I'll take every wild and crazy minute with you I can get. Whenever. Wherever."

He waited so long to answer, Becka thought he would reject her offer outright and send her away for good. Her heart trip-hammered against her rib cage.

Then, when she was ready to give up, his head dropped backward and he let out a victory whoop.

"Come here, woman." He pulled her toward him. "Watch the knee. The sharks are back." The old familiar grin kicked up. "So you're willing to settle for a few hot nights and fun-filled days?"

She nodded. "Anything."

"Not me, darlin'. I want all of you, every day, for always. That is, if you can put up with a one-legged cowboy who sings in his sleep."

She raised her head, staring into his gorgeous eyes. "Are you serious?"

"Scary, ain't it?" He rocked her back and forth, chuckling. After a minute he stopped and grew serious. His warm breath brushed the side of her face.

"I learned a thing or two myself today. All my life, I've feared commitment as much as you feared danger. I thought I didn't have staying power, that I lacked something other men had. But when I saw Dylan at the bottom of that ravine, I realized what my heart had been trying to tell me all along. Commitment is loving somebody so much that you'd do anything for them. That's how I feel about you and Dylan. I love you, too, Becka-Rebecka."

Tilting her lips to his, he kissed her tenderly. Joy, sweet and powerful, flooded her soul.

"I love you so much I can't stand it."

"Good. Then you'll forgive me for not getting down on one knee to do this."

She smiled, relishing the strength of his arms around her, thrilled that the man she loved, loved her in return. "What are you talking about, you wonderful, loony man?

"This." He kissed her again. Then when she was certain she would combust, he lifted his head. Eyes dancing, he asked, "B. Washburn, RN, will you marry me?"

Unable to contain her relief and happiness, Becka laughed out loud. Then, immediately contrite, she pressed a kiss to his lips. "I'm so sorry. I shouldn't laugh. Your knee…"

"Forget the knee. Will you marry me or not?"

"Oh, yes. I absolutely will."

"Good. Now kiss me and make me all better."

And so she did.

Epilogue

Watching his bride come toward him, down the aisle of the Rattlesnake Chapel, Jett's chest expanded like a hot-air balloon. He'd parasailed behind a motorboat, hang glided off the side of a mountain, and free-fallen from an airplane, but nothing could compare to the rush he experienced at the sight of his Becka.

In a long, off-the-shoulder gown the color of champagne, his red-haired bride was a vision, a dream—the dream he wanted more than anything.

Funny how he'd fought against falling in love, and now he realized loving and being loved was the best thing that could happen to a person.

As the swell of music subsided, Becka reached his side. He winked, and she returned the favor with a tremulous, glossy-eyed smile. Her sweet perfume, mixed with the scent of pink roses, wrapped around him.

He couldn't believe all the changes in his life in the past five months. Changes that filled him with a contentment and joy he'd never had.

He'd taken over the wheeling and dealing aspect of the ranch that Colt despised, leaving the day-to-day work to his brother. And to his surprise, he enjoyed it, just as he would enjoy settling down with Becka in the new house he'd built on ranch land.

And he'd battled back from another surgery, thanks to Becka. She'd badgered and pushed and sweated along with him until he'd regained more use of his knee than any surgeon ever expected.

And next to Becka, the best change of all came in the form of a four-year-old who dogged his every footstep. He glanced down at the child between them. Standing stiff and straight in his dinner suit, he gripped the wedding rings with fierce responsibility. No longer timid and confused, Dylan, his buddy, his son, was a joy.

The preacher said something then, and Jett turned his thoughts to the moment he'd never expected to experience. The ceremony flew by in a blur. When the preacher asked if he would take Rebecka as his wife, all he could think was yes, yes, yes.

The reception hall was filled to overflowing with friends and family who'd come to witness what none of them believed would ever happen.

Becka held her hand out and gazed with unbridled joy at the wedding ring on her third finger and then up at the gorgeous cowboy beside her. She was Mrs. Jett Garrett, the happiest woman on planet Earth. She still couldn't believe it any more than she could believe that

Jett had sung to her during the ceremony. She'd cried like a baby and ruined her carefully applied makeup.

Teeth flashing, Jett slipped an arm around her and then held his own hand next to hers. A gold band sparkled in the light.

"Looks good, huh? A perfectly matched set. Just like us."

Wearing a black dinner suit with a vest that matched her dress, he took her breath away. As he bent to kiss her, for at least the tenth time in the last ten minutes, she tasted celebratory wine and a healthy dose of desire. Her blood heated with pleasure and she let the feeling flow, free at last to be who she was. All fear and guilt had vanished in the strength and security of Jett's love for her and Dylan.

Coming up beside them, Colt cleared his throat.

With his usual mischievous expression, Jett looked up. "Go away, brother. You've got your own woman."

"If you two are going to stand around here and kiss all day, you'll miss your plane."

Jett checked his watch. "You're right. Thanks, bro. Time to blow this joint, Mrs. Garrett." He gave her a saucy wink.

Someone tugged on the hem of her wedding gown.

"Mama. When are you and Dad leaving?" Dylan's freckled nose wrinkled impatiently. "Evan and me gots stuff to do."

Since he'd discovered he would be staying with Kati and Colt while the newlyweds went on a honeymoon, he'd been eager to get this wedding over with.

"As a matter of fact, we're on our way. Give me a kiss."

With an exaggerated sigh, he thrust his face forward

and allowed a smooch. Becka enveloped him and said, "Be good."

Leaving him, even for a few days, was still hard for her.

Jett took a turn next, hauling the child into his arms for a giant hug. "Promise you'll mind Kati, and next month we'll all take a trip somewhere especially for kids."

"Okay!" Wiggling down, he said. "I gotta tell Evan. Bye, Mama. Bye, Dad."

While Jett beamed with fatherly pride, Becka fought a tear.

"No more crying, Becka-Rebecka. I'm getting a complex."

"As if you could." She slugged his shoulder.

"Mosquito bite." He laughed, rubbing the spot. "Ready for our honeymoon trip?"

He'd kept the destination a secret, promising a surprise she'd love. The anticipation had been part of the fun.

"Don't you think you'd better tell me where we're going now?"

"I told you to pack your swimsuit."

"And?"

He tapped her on the nose. "How about shark diving in Mexico."

"What?" She slapped a hand against her chest, jabbing the pearl appliqués into her skin.

Jett's head tipped back in a hearty laugh. "Just joking. We'll save that for an anniversary."

"We certainly will." As glad as she was to once more enjoy the thought of water sports, she wasn't quite ready for sharks.

"Will you settle for night snorkeling with the manta

rays off the Florida Keys?" He dropped his voice to a sexy whisper. "And maybe a little underwater night snuggling, as well."

Her blood raced with exhilaration. Living life to the fullest never felt so good. "Yes, to both."

On tiptoe, she kissed him again.

"Yummy." He traced her lips with one finger. "You want to try that again?"

"Absolutely." She did.

When they parted, Jett snugged her close and growled, "Let's forget Florida and head to the nearest motel."

"Not on your life, cowboy."

"Spoilsport."

With a saucy grin, she walked her fingers up his chest and purred, "I'll make it up to you when we get there."

A naughty gleam leaped to his eyes. "I'm going to hold you to that."

"You'd better."

With a spurt of surprised laughter, he captured her hand and bowed toward the exit. "Our carriage awaits."

They ran out the door and down the steps through a gauntlet of laughing, cheering well-wishers. Bird seed peppered them.

As they reached the curb where she'd expected to find his pickup waiting, Becka froze. A motorcycle the size of a horse was there instead. Streamers rippling from the handlebars, a Just Married sign was tied to the back.

Jett made a grand sweeping motion with one hand. "Well? What do you think?"

From an inner pocket he took a pair of wraparound sunglasses and slid them on. After handing her a pair, he tossed an elegantly clad leg over the bike and raised his eyebrows in question.

"I think you're insane, but I love you, anyway." Scooping her full satin skirt into one hand, she climbed on behind him.

With one gleaming Italian leather shoe, he kick-started the Harley and revved the engine.

"Hang on, darlin'. You're in for a ride."

With a heart full of trust and love, Becka wrapped her arms around her husband's waist and squealed with excitement as the bike pulled away.

Life with Jett Garrett would always be an exhilarating ride.

And Becka didn't plan to miss a minute of it.

* * * * *

SILHOUETTE *Romance*®

First comes love...
then comes marriage?

Hunter Starnes had once run from his small-town roots *and* his love for his childhood sweetheart—but he wasn't that man anymore. And Claire Dent was no longer a young girl who believed in the magic of rainbows. She was an alluring woman who deserved a ring, a promise and a family. But could the man who had stolen her dreams be the one to offer her everything?

A RING AND A RAINBOW
by **Deanna Talcott**
Silhouette Romance #1753

On sale January 2005!

Only from Silhouette Books!

If you enjoyed what you just read,
then we've got an offer you can't resist!

Take 2 bestselling
love stories FREE!
Plus get a FREE surprise gift!

Clip this page and mail it to Silhouette Reader Service™

IN U.S.A.	**IN CANADA**
3010 Walden Ave.	P.O. Box 609
P.O. Box 1867	Fort Erie, Ontario
Buffalo, N.Y. 14240-1867	L2A 5X3

YES! Please send me 2 free Silhouette Romance® novels and my free surprise gift. After receiving them, if I don't wish to receive anymore, I can return the shipping statement marked cancel. If I don't cancel, I will receive 4 brand-new novels every month, before they're available in stores! In the U.S.A., bill me at the bargain price of $3.57 plus 25¢ shipping and handling per book and applicable sales tax, if any*. In Canada, bill me at the bargain price of $4.05 plus 25¢ shipping and handling per book and applicable taxes**. That's the complete price and a savings of at least 10% off the cover prices—what a great deal! I understand that accepting the 2 free books and gift places me under no obligation ever to buy any books. I can always return a shipment and cancel at any time. Even if I never buy another book from Silhouette, the 2 free books and gift are mine to keep forever.

210 SDN DZ7L
310 SDN DZ7M

Name _____ (PLEASE PRINT)

Address _____ Apt.#

City _____ State/Prov. _____ Zip/Postal Code

Not valid to current Silhouette Romance® subscribers.

Want to try two free books from another series?
Call 1-800-873-8635 or visit www.morefreebooks.com.

* Terms and prices subject to change without notice. Sales tax applicable in N.Y.
** Canadian residents will be charged applicable provincial taxes and GST.
All orders subject to approval. Offer limited to one per household.
® are registered trademarks owned and used by the trademark owner and or its licensee.

SROM04R   ©2004 Harlequin Enterprises Limited